## 'How do you know for sure that you couldn't have a baby?'

'Well, I…don't know for sure, of course,' she said, her voice low and her cheeks burning. Hopefully he could not see that too clearly.

Guy eased himself round so that he was facing her, very close. Josey wanted to touch his face, to trace the outline of his mouth with her fingers.

'Forgive me if I sound facetious, Josey, I don't mean to be. If you want to know if you can become pregnant, it could be fun finding out.'

'And what would happen then?' she ventured.

'I would be prepared for the consequences,' he said, with a slow smile that totally disarmed her at that moment. Her face flamed with her own thoughts of wanting him. 'It doesn't matter so much, you know, Josey. A man could love you for yourself, without that.'

**Rebecca Lang** trained to be a State Registered Nurse in Kent, England, where she was born. Her main focus of interest became operating theatre work, and she gained extensive experience in all types of surgery on both sides of the Atlantic. Now living in Vancouver, Canada, she is married to a Canadian pathologist and has three children. When not writing, Rebecca enjoys gardening, reading, theatre, exploring new places, and anything to do with the study of people.

**Recent titles by the same author:**

# A BABY
# FOR JOSEY

### BY
### REBECCA LANG

*First published in Great Britain 2001
Harlequin Mills & Boon Limited,
Eton House, 18-24 Paradise Road, Richmond, Surrey TW9 1SR*

© Rebecca Lang 2001

0 263 82683 X

*Set in Times Roman 10½ on 12 pt.
03-0801-54011*

*Printed and bound in Spain
by Litografia Rosés, S.A., Barcelona*

# CHAPTER ONE

'MY GOD, chaos as usual!' Josey Lincoln, RN, muttered to herself as she went through the second set of double swing doors into the wide main lobby of the emergency department of Gresham General Hospital, Gresham, Ontario. This hospital, together with the other major teaching hospital downtown, the University Hospital, dealt with most of the more serious medical emergencies that occurred in downtown Gresham and beyond.

'Why should I expect it to be any different?' She went on talking to herself as she speeded up, heading towards the nurses' locker room. She was 'getting into stride,' as she called it, mentally gearing up for the onslaught that she knew would be her lot for the next eight hours of the day shift.

It was still dark outside, as it always was at 7 a.m. on a January morning. There was heavy snow, a fresh fall having come down in the night, and as she walked she brushed snowflakes off her sheepskin coat. She felt a familiar rising tide of frustration overtaking her as she looked around at the patients waiting to be seen, some sitting, some standing, some pacing with family members or friends. The majority would be lying on stretchers out of sight, and some were in full view in the corridors.

Basically Josey loved her job, knew without conceit that she was good at it. Yet she also knew that if you didn't pace yourself carefully, didn't look after yourself, didn't treat yourself right first and foremost, it would get you. The stress, that was—if not the patients. Gresham was a tough city in parts, and Gresham General was near some of those parts, with a grimy underbelly that they, the staff, were privileged to witness day in and day out—not to mention night in and night out.

Maybe she had come back too early after her bout of flu, only having taken a week off. Maybe that accounted for the sinking feeling she now felt. And maybe talking to yourself was a sign of impending madness, as everyone said it was, she thought with a wry grin as she turned her key to open the door to the locker room that was situated in a small side corridor away from the patient areas. It was easy to think that you might be losing your sanity in these days of gross cutbacks in funding to hospitals, when so many trained nurses had been laid off and beds closed that the situation could become dangerous.

Automatically she went through the motions of turning the dial of the combination lock on her locker, then changing into a pale blue two-piece scrub suit and white lace-up running shoes. Round her neck she hung a pen on a cord, put her stethoscope, notebook, pen-light and other accoutrements into a capacious pocket of the loose-fitting top.

As she left the locker room she felt the familiar churning inside—part excitement, part apprehension—that she always felt at the beginning of each working shift, even after the years she had put in there. The problems she had been thinking about were familiar ones, which had been gone over ad nauseam by herself and her colleagues. Those trained nurses who were left to carry the load were working constantly very close to breaking-point.

Next stop was the departmental coffee-room. She had about ten minutes in which to drink a welcome cup of coffee and have a quick chat with her colleagues before she looked at the assignment sheet for the day to find out which area of the department she would be working in. Knowing the head nurse—Selina Macintosh, known generally as Mac—as she did, she would be given a choice as this was her first day back after being sick.

The coffee-room, not far from the locker room and away from the patient areas, was bustling with staff when she entered—nurses, doctors, orderlies, porters, technicians, two or three medical students—getting a last-minute shot of caffeine to set them up for the next few hours. There were two large coffee-urns which were replenished throughout the day. Some of the local bakeries donated muffins, doughnuts and bread rolls. In this place you never knew when you would next get to eat.

'Good morning, Josey.' She was greeted immediately by Selina. 'How are you?' The head nurse stood near the door, sipping from an oversized cup.

'Not bad.' Josey smiled at her as she opened a cupboard to get out her own coffee-mug and proceeded to get herself coffee. 'I've been better, but I think I'll last the day.'

'I'm giving you a choice—you can have ambulatory care, medical emergency or Surgical Trauma. I would give you the triage station if I could, but we're operating with a skeleton staff so I need you elsewhere. This flu bug that's doing the rounds has just about done us in. For every person I've got working, I've got one who isn't working, and just about every third patient has the flu, with pneumonia thrown in.'

'Well...' Josey said, 'I'll take surgical trauma.' She took a swallow of coffee. 'Ah, that's better.'

'Good for you,' Mac said approvingly.

They both knew that while the surgical trauma section of the ER could put a nurse in a situation where all hell could break loose, especially if there was a major catastrophe, there were periods between of relative calm while they dealt with the resulting mess and set up the one particular room for the next case. There were three trauma rooms, each set up like an operating room with everything that could possibly be needed. She would be working in one of them, with one other registered nurse. Alternatively, in the medical emergency section, especially at epidemic time, there was a never-ending stream of seriously ill patients, with heart attacks, influenza, pneumonia and many other conditions, some common, some obscure.

Mac was an ideal individual for her role as head nurse. With her calm, shrewd, no-nonsense personality, coupled with her skills as an emergency nurse, few could browbeat her or get the better of her in a confrontation, especially when she was defending her nursing staff. Josey admired and respected her. It had been Mac who had listened to her when she had been through that awful time of breaking up with Joe, when she had felt that the bottom had been falling out of her life and she had been in some kind of vortex. Nothing had been sure then, everything in a state of flux, with her confidence at a very low ebb.

'Just be glad you're not married to him.' That had been one of the things Mac had said to her then. 'And that you don't have any children. Think of how much more com-plicated it would be.'

Ever practical, the head nurse had helped her to view her situation as something other than the total disaster she her-self had thought it to be.

'If you break up after two years of living with someone,' Mac had continued, 'you weren't meant to be together. That's a good testing period.'

That had been eighteen months ago...

Someone came into the coffee-room behind Josey as she stood with her back to the door, breaking into her obsessive reverie. Even after all that time, she still thought of Joe at least once a day.

'By the way,' Mac was saying to her now, as she tried to drag her mind back to the present, 'while you were away sick, Dr Ramsay had a skiing accident, broke a leg. He's OK, but won't be with us for some time.'

'Oh, no! That's all we need,' Josey said, surprised. 'No one told me.'

Dr Alec Ramsay was the head of the emergency department. A middle-aged man, he was very good at his job, in all three roles of doctor, teacher and administrator to the department.

'Have we got a replacement?' she asked, speculating on how on earth they would manage without Dr Ramsay.

'Yes, we've got Dr Guy Lake, who's just spent a year at University Hospital,' the head nurse informed her.

'Dr Ramsay's a hard act to follow,' Josey commented, thinking that she would miss the kindly doctor and that she wouldn't relish working with someone new who would most likely only be there until Dr Ramsay was fit again.

Someone behind her cleared his throat, and Mac shifted her gaze from Josey's face to a point just over her shoulder.

'Oh, Dr Lake,' she said sweetly, 'meet another of my nurses. This is Josey Lincoln, RN, who's been off sick for a week.'

Feeling a slight flush of embarrassment at having implied that no one could take the place of Dr Ramsay, which he must have heard, Josey turned round slowly, expecting to see someone about the same age as Alec Ramsay, tired, overworked, pale, with a droopy face like a bloodhound.

Instead, she saw a tall, muscular man, broad-shouldered, something of the male counterpart of Mac, who was a strongly built woman. He was pale, to be sure, but considerably younger than Alec Ramsay and not as chronically exhausted. He had thick, dark hair, a little too long, that curled up rakishly at the back where it met the collar of the white lab coat that he wore over a green scrub suit.

Josey's eyes met his and, with a sense of shock, she felt her flush deepening. His eyes were blue-grey, coolly appraising. He didn't smile.

'Yes,' he said, 'Alec Ramsay is a hard act to follow. We've worked together.' The voice was pleasant, low, with a soothing quality which Josey felt sure would be appreciated by the patients who came into the ER.

'Um…' she said. It wasn't often that she felt tongue-tied. In fact, a ready riposte was seldom far from her lips, a faculty that was well honed in the department where one had to deal with all comers. Yet this man who stood before her left her momentarily nonplussed. He was very attractive.

Having a man affect her in this way wasn't common since she had split up with Joe. Most men left her cold, and that was the way she wanted it for a good long time. The emotional numbness, after the storm of emotion had swept by, had been a welcome feeling to her, like an insulating barrier. She felt herself half wishing that the new doctor had been an elderly, droopy bloodhound, a kindly back-patting sort of a guy, the type who would call her 'honey' without being patronizing…so long as he was good at his job. Then she wouldn't have to think about how much she was really missing being with a specific man.

Guy Lake, she thought as she looked at him, had that rare combination of the sophisticated, intelligent professional man and the physicality of the bricklayer. He seemed to exude an understated manliness, a ready-for-anything persona which, it seemed to her, included dealing with women in all their aspects. For some unaccountable reason, she shivered.

'You've had the flu bug?' he asked her, his eyebrows

slightly raised, as though he really cared about her state of health.

'Yes…'

'This particular one is unusually virulent, it seems,' he said. 'It certainly doesn't pay to neglect it. I've seen patients with quite bad secondary pneumonia and a few with encephalitis—sometimes both. Never neglect flu, Ms Lincoln, never neglect a sore throat, or any sort of viral infection.'

'Um…no. I try not to,' Josey agreed. 'I would have preferred a month off. And maybe a holiday in the West Indies as well.'

'That's a thought,' he said.

'Well,' Mac said, squeezing past Josey, looking her full in the face, 'it's back to the fray for me.' It seemed to Josey that there was a meaningful light in her eyes, a quick, subtle message for her, woman to woman. 'Now…' Mac addressed herself to Dr Lake, 'you be gentle with Josey today, Dr Lake, since she's been sick. She's working with you in surgical trauma. She's one of my best nurses.'

'I'm always gentle, Ms Macintosh,' he said.

'I'll keep you to that,' Mac said. 'She has a good brain, that one. And they don't all come that way, believe me. I get some who are a few bales short of a load.'

This time Dr Lake allowed a glimmer of amusement to enter his cool eyes. 'I'll hold her hand if necessary,' he said.

'Great,' she said, moving off.

Still he didn't smile at Josey, simply looked at her and the colour on her cheeks, his attractive, chiselled mouth set in a straight line. Perhaps he suffered from that same occupational cynicism that affected her, Josey thought. Yet there was a dynamism about him, an energy waiting to be let loose, it seemed.

'Does Mac come from a farming background?' he enquired, deadpan. 'I've never asked her.'

'I believe so,' Josey said, surprised at the sudden change in tack. So he had a sense of humour. One mark in his favour.

'Josey...' he said speculatively. 'Is that short for Joanne?'

'No, it's Josephine,' she said, recovering her composure. 'My mother was reading a biography of Napoleon when she was pregnant with me.'

'Ah,' he said. He looked searchingly at the young woman before him, at the slightly flushed, smooth skin, at the smattering of freckles over the nose, at the generous mouth, the greeny eyes, and the light brown hair that had hints of red in it. 'A good thing you didn't turn out to be a boy.'

'Maybe,' she said, smiling slightly, aware of the grudging nature of her own smile, for no other reason than that he was a male of a certain category. Joe, after all, had been an ER doctor too, so that was the excuse for her reticence. Guy Lake had nothing to do with him, with any of that, yet the emotions running riot through her often seemed to have no obvious logic to them, or at least none that was immediately discernible.

One of the surgical interns in the room handed Dr Lake a mug of coffee. 'Thanks,' he said.

Josey noticed how large his hands were, large and capable, with long fingers and well-shaped, short, clean nails. They inspired confidence in her; she could imagine him being capable of dealing with anything and everything that came into the ER. Whatever else he turned out to be, she felt sure he wouldn't be a wimp.

Over the rim of the mug, as he took a swallow of the coffee, Guy Lake regarded Josey Lincoln. Most men, he reflected, appreciated intelligence, a sense of humour and independence in a woman, first and foremost. Although physical attractiveness first made a man notice a woman, that paled to insignificance if she wasn't intelligent...then interest faded.

This young woman appeared to have all four attributes— if one could make such a quick assessment. She had to be of independent mind in order to have taken on the job she was doing. Over the years, in this demanding and often brutal job, he had become pretty good at assessing people in a hurry, although he had also learnt not to act immediately on such a hasty assessment where his colleagues were concerned.

'I'm very sorry about Dr Ramsay,' Josey said. 'Is he all right?'

'Yes. He's at University Hospital, being well cared for.'

'Good. I'm going to miss him.' Josey drank her coffee hurriedly, looking at the clock. Almost time to go.

'Perhaps I can compensate,' he said.

For no reason that she could understand, Josey felt the colour rising again in her cheeks. I must be frustrated, she thought, if a simple remark from a man can be that significant.

There were things she wanted to know about Dr Lake— where he came from, where he had worked—which she could hardly ask him directly at a first meeting. No doubt the grapevine would inform her pretty quickly. Although he was younger than Alec Ramsay, there was a seasoned quality about him.

'Hey, Josey!' Another registered nurse, Brian Todd, known as just Todd or Toddy, called to her from the doorway as he was going out. 'We're working together. See you in there.'

'OK, Todd,' she called back, smiling. 'Coming.' Relieved that she was working with someone she really liked, with whom she worked well as a two-person team—which wasn't always the case with some of the more abrasive characters on the staff—she swallowed the last few mouthfuls of her coffee, still standing beside Guy, more than ordinarily aware of him physically. That unwelcome awareness irritated her. Now she could focus on Todd, with whom she felt comfortable, like easing one's aching feet into old, familiar shoes.

Todd, one of three male nurses in the department, was a great asset, good to work with. Competent at his job, he was also big enough physically, adept and energetic, to be able to deal with the more difficult patients who arrived there—the abusive drug addicts, the alcoholics, the homeless mentally ill, or the merely short-tempered.

'Excuse me. Must go,' she said to Guy, smiling awkwardly. It wouldn't do to let him get a hint that she found him as attractive as, probably, did every other woman in the department. For I am damaged goods...

He nodded.

It was with a strange sense of relief that she joined Brian Todd, the familiar presence, after being in the company of a man, however briefly, who seemed very much an unknown quantity to her, engendering in her a feeling of dissonance. That feeling made her realize how emotionally fragile she had become.

She didn't want to come out of that self-imposed exile where men were concerned, away from that protective cynicism which had been with her for a long time. Dr Guy Lake was attractive in a very disturbing way, and she had found in those few moments that she couldn't stand back and look at him dispassionately. The thought frightened her. And there was certainly no way of avoiding him. Another thing—he was probably very married, with three or four children. You could usually tell; there was a certain detachment about a man. Guy Lake certainly had that detachment, in spite of a light-hearted side, apparently. Not that it would really mean anything to her, of course, one way or the other...

'How are you, Josey? I missed you,' Toddy queried as she came up to him breathlessly in the side corridor.

'Actually, not really back to par, Todd,' she said truthfully, 'but well enough, I hope.'

'Let's hope it isn't "one of those days", then,' he said cheerfully, although she knew that he relished those days.

Josey shrugged as they hurried towards the surgical trauma area of the ER. 'Best not to think about it, Toddy,' she said. 'One step at a time, one case at a time.'

'My sentiments exactly,' he agreed. 'What's the point of dwelling on lack of staff, lack of money, when there's you and me, Josey?'

Josey laughed as she hurried to keep up with him. Todd was tall and sandy-haired, with very pale eyebrows and eyelashes that made his face look naked. He had an open personality to match, as well as a wicked sense of humour which helped them all to keep their spirits up when it looked as though they would never get through the load of work.

'What's the new doc like, Todd?'

'Good, very good,' Todd said sombrely, a trifle grudgingly, no doubt thinking about Dr Ramsay and his fractured leg.

'That's a relief,' she said.

'I never thought I'd say that, having worked with Alec Ramsay,' Todd went on. 'Dr Lake's got a good personality, too—calm, you know, like he should be for this place. He knows exactly what he has to do, and just does it. No fuss, no bother.'

'Mmm.'

'He's quiet,' Todd added. 'Doesn't talk about himself. He came from University Hospital, he was second in command there, fully trained in trauma.'

At the trauma area they both went into the first room, which would be their domain for the day. It was routine first thing in the morning to check the room to make sure that all the equipment was in place, clean or sterile and ready to go. There would be two registered nurses in each of the other two trauma rooms.

The department had thirty-four beds for patients waiting to be treated; when these were full, patients were put on stretchers and left in the corridors. Patients for surgical trauma came in by ambulance. They weren't in any condition to wait, so came straight to the rooms where they would be treated.

Apart from Guy, there were two other staff doctors, twelve registered nurses, at least one resident doctor training in ER medicine, several orderlies, a few technicians, porters, a medical student or two, as well as the security staff and the admitting clerks. Other specialized medical staff were called in when needed. They all scrambled to treat this flood of people. They could have used double the number of nurses and many more doctors.

Just as they were finishing the check of the room the buzzer sounded on the internal telephone, which meant a call from the front triage station where all incoming patients were assessed and placed in a category according to urgency.

'Here we go,' Todd said, lifting the receiver.

Josey put on a long plastic apron, some paper overshoes, and a soft paper cap over her hair. In the pocket of her uniform she had a pair of plastic goggles to protect her eyes against splashes of blood that could possibly carry the deadly AIDS virus and hepatitis.

'Right…right.' Todd was saying, as he jotted down a few things on a notepad. Josey opened some bags of IV fluid.

He replaced the receiver of the telephone and took a deep breath. 'Man coming in with multiple stab wounds, hypothermia, fractured leg and arm, probable fractured ribs, breathing problem, head injury and probable internal abdominal injury. Found down at the waterfront…beaten up, pushed into the water, probably drug-related…multiple lacerations to the face.' He stopped, letting out his breath with an exaggerated whooshing sound, and he and Josey looked at each other.

'Surprising he didn't freeze to death in about ten seconds,' Josey commented.

'According to the police, someone witnessed the attack, pulled him out and called the police and ambulance, then disappeared as soon as he saw the police coming,' Todd said. 'Otherwise he would have frozen, which was maybe what someone intended.'

Josey shook her head. 'I get the picture,' she said. 'Let's open a few packs, Todd.'

'He's going to be here within ten minutes,' Todd added. 'Have we got an IV nurse here today, do you know? Or are they all off sick with the flu?' As he spoke he whizzed around the room, getting stuff ready.

'I saw Sandeep,' Josey said, naming one of the nurses whose job it was to insert intravenous lines on their patients, among other things.

The anaesthesia resident came into the room. 'Hi, guys,' he said. 'How goes it?'

'Morning, Dr Leum,' Josey and Todd greeted him in unison.

'We're right on track,' Josey added, rushing about as

though she and Todd were partners in a well-rehearsed dance, 'and raring to go.'

Dr Bill Leum went straight over to the anaesthetic machine and began to check his equipment. 'Sounds like I'll have to intubate this guy.'

They knew when their patient was coming by the sounds of raised voices and activity in the corridor. Todd and Josey both moved to swing open the double doors to the room.

The stretcher bearing their patient was manoeuvred expertly through the doors by the two burly paramedics who were dressed in warm, bulky clothes against the extreme cold outside. Josey stood back to allow them through, feeling the adrenaline surging through her body, readying her for action.

'Morning, Josephine,' one of the paramedics said to her, giving her a wink as he came into the room, letting loose a flurry of snowflakes that had clung to his jacket. 'How's my girl?'

'Just great, Alan,' Josey said as she moved forward with the patient. 'How's yourself?'

'Just dandy,' he said, 'which is more than I can say for this guy. Right. One, two, three…heave!'

Their patient's face was deathly pale. Josey looked at him for the first time as they positioned him on the operating table. There was a decided grey tinge to the skin. His nose and mouth were covered by an oxygen mask. Dried blood matted his hair and caked part of his face. The eyelids were swollen and blue. The remainder of his body was swaddled in blankets, and an IV tube snaked down under them at one end.

'We have a warming blanket,' Todd said. 'Does anyone know how long he was in the water?'

'No,' one of the paramedics said. 'Couldn't have been very long, and most of the lake's frozen. There must have been a warm spot.' He was referring to Lake Ontario, which bordered the south side of Gresham. 'He's in a bad way.'

'Easy does it,' Bill Leum said, as they all helped to re-move the blankets and replace them with an automatic warming blanket, with Josey supporting the fractured arm which was padded and splinted, while Todd supported the fractured leg.

At that moment Dr Guy Lake came in through the op-posite door, having been divested of his white lab coat, and Josey glanced at him quickly, uncommonly aware of his presence. Calmly he looked at the patient, taking in the scene, then he took goggles out of his pocket and put them on, then a pair of latex gloves from a pile, and a plastic apron.

'I thought I'd intubate him, Dr Lake,' the anaesthesia resident said. 'He's unconscious.'

'Yes, go ahead. I'd like a Swan-Ganz catheter put in, and two more IVs. We may have to cut down to put those in, by the look of it. And I'd like him to have an oesopha-geal temperature probe,' Dr Lake said. 'And call me Guy. We may as well be on a first-name basis here.'

'Right,' Bill Leum said. A third-year medical student had come in to help him and to learn, and was standing by somewhat apprehensively. Josey gave him a quick, en-couraging smile.

'We get the monitor leads on first, for his vital signs,' she said to him quietly.

Sandeep, the IV nurse, had come into the room also. After conferring briefly with Bill, she got to work to get more intravenous lines in position. If anyone could get a needle in a vein, she could.

Guy turned to Josey. 'Right, team,' he said, 'let's go.'

Todd moved quickly to cut off what remained of their patient's clothing, while the others set to work, going through the usual step-by-step routine to save the man's life, if it was humanly possible to save it.

'Can you help to get the cardiac monitor on, Josey, and the blood-pressure cuff, while I do the intubation?' Bill said.

'Sure. I've got the IV plasma set up in the warmer,' Josey said, moving into action, feeling Guy's eyes on her. The patient's breathing was laboured—the sooner they got that tube in his trachea, the better.

'Do your thing, Sandeep,' Guy said to the IV nurse, standing beside the table. 'Let's get some circulating fluid in him. We'll start with the Ringer's and the plasma, then get onto the O-neg blood.'

They could all see from the monitor that both temperature and blood pressure were dangerously low.

'We haven't got a name,' one of the paramedics said from the doorway as they prepared to move their equipment out. 'He had no ID on him, nothing. That's why the police think he was done over deliberately.'

With that parting information, which the others took without comment, the two paramedics backed out of the room with their stretcher and oxygen tanks.

Moments later an X-ray technologist came in, tying on a face mask. 'Morning,' he said. 'What can I do for you?'

'Just take a straight shot of the chest first,' Guy said to him, 'then the skull, please, then the left arm and leg. Then can we get organized for a CT scan before he goes to the operating rooms?' As he spoke he shone a bright light from his ophthalmoscope into the patient's eyes. According to how the pupils reacted to light, he could partially assess the degree of brain damage.

'Sure,' the technician said, beginning to roll out his heavy equipment from behind sliding doors.

Each member of staff went about his or her appointed task quickly and efficiently, yet without undue haste.

'Josey.' Guy looked at her, straightening up from listening to the man's chest with his stethoscope. 'Would you help me insert the chest tube? It sounds as though we might need more than one—one for drainage and one to let the air out. We won't wait for the X-ray film to come back. Todd, could you prepare the abdomen for the mini-laparotomy?'

'OK, Dr Lake—Guy,' Todd said, having just about finished cutting off the clothing. In doing the mini-laparotomy, a simple, effective procedure that could be done in ten minutes, they could find out if there was bleeding in the abdominal cavity.

'And can someone put in a call for an orthopaedic staff man, please?' Guy said. 'I want someone to look at those fractures, stat. By the look of the blood pressure, there may be bleeding from those—maybe the femoral artery.'

'I'll do it,' Todd said. 'Right away.' He pushed the equipment into place so that the ER resident could make a start, then hurried over to the internal telephone.

'Have we got any blood ready?' Guy asked.

'Yeah, it's all taken care of,' Bill said. 'Should be here any minute. He's getting the plasma and the Ringer's, and we're just putting up the O-neg.'

'Get that blood pressure up,' Guy said tersely, 'or we'll all be wasting our time.'

'It's better than it was,' Bill said, juggling with syringes and IV lines, injecting drugs into the rubber ports on the lines. 'I've put in a call for Jerry Wong,' he added, referring to the staff anaesthetist who was skilled in trauma work.

Josey pushed over the trolley containing the sterile equipment for insertion of a chest tube. After another quick glance at the patient's face, Josey didn't look at it again, but concentrated on the small area that was of immediate concern.

The ER resident-in-training, Doug Randall, came into the room. 'What would you like me to do first?' he asked, putting on his gear, all set to following Guy's instructions. There was no conversation as such, only the necessary communication as each person bent to his or her task.

'Wow, what a mess!' Josey said feelingly to Guy, as they worked side by side. It was obvious, now that his coverings were off, that this unknown man had been very badly beaten.

'Yes,' he agreed. 'These stab wounds looked relatively superficial, but they're oozing blood steadily. He must have been partially protected in the assault by that thick jacket he was wearing. Just as well, otherwise he would have been a DOA for sure.' They looked at the multiple lacerations and bruising all over their patient's body.

He appeared to be about thirty-five years of age, although it was difficult to tell—he could have been much younger, Josey speculated as she took off her unsterile rubber gloves and put on a sterile pair. Beyond that, she didn't speculate too much. As always, she felt a deep, poignant sadness and empathy for people like him, wondering about his life history, about the circumstances that had brought him to this point where he was hovering close to death. Mercifully, he was completely out of it.

'Do you mind if I call you Josey?' Guy asked quietly as he stood next to her, putting his large hands, size eight, into sterile gloves.

'Please, do,' she said. Looking at him, acknowledging then that she had avoided meeting his eyes for more than a few seconds up to now, she was jolted back into an acute awareness of him as an attractive man. She had certainly felt him looking at her since he had entered the room.

His intelligent, perceptive eyes looked into hers over the top of his surgical mask so that for a few seconds her attention was arrested, as though they were the only two in the room. She knew beyond a shadow of a doubt that he knew precisely what she had been thinking and feeling about the man. 'You wonder how people get to this state, don't you?' he said.

'Yes,' she said. The new doctor seemed to know that she needed that understanding.

'Ready?' he said, lifting his eyebrows slightly.

Josey nodded. 'Yes.'

All at once she was oddly glad of this doctor's large physical presence beside her, glad that she was working closely with him, even though she mistrusted any such feelings. This was where she had met Joe, and she had had very similar feelings then...

She concentrated totally on the job as they prepared to insert chest tubes.

'Thanks, Josey,' Guy said quietly, after he had made the first incision in the chest wall and she had handed him the first tube for insertion. 'After this, we shall almost certainly have to do burr holes. I don't think I want to wait until we can get him to the operating room. He has a subarachnoid haemorrhage, judging by the uneven size of his pupils. I want to see the skull X-rays before I make a start.'

'Right,' Josey said. 'We have everything ready for burr holes.' The bleeding inside the skull would be the result of a fracture or from blows to the head, she speculated. Blood would be accumulating, pressing on the brain, the pressure building up dangerously. That pressure, she knew, had to be relieved by the drilling of at least one small hole in the skull to let out the blood. Before doing that, they had to locate the exact area of the haemorrhage...

The atmosphere was tense as the case proceeded. They

had two chest tubes in place. Doug Randall and Todd had put in a urinary catheter in short order and were well into doing the mini-lap.

'There's blood here,' Doug said, siphoning back the saline solution from the abdominal cavity, which came back red. 'Quite a lot of it.'

'No surprise,' Guy said. 'We need to ship him out the minute he's stable.'

A voice came over the intercom from the triage station. 'We have an orthopaedic staff man and a neurosurgeon on their way here, Dr Lake. That's Dr Cox and Dr Lindman. Dr Jerry Wong's already here.'

'Roger,' Todd said from his position on the other side of the operating table where he and Doug were working.

'Josey,' Guy said, straightening up, 'can you scrub out and get on to the operating room—tell them what's what? We'll transfer him there as soon as I've done the burr holes. You know the routine.'

'Yes,' she said, stripping off her gloves and heading to the telephone.

At that moment Jerry Wong came into the room, ready for action. He was small, thin and wiry, a tireless man, so it always seemed to Josey.

'What's going on?' he said to her. In a few moments she had given him the patient's history, what little they knew, and told him where they were in his treatment. He nodded and joined his colleague, Bill, at the head of the operating table.

'Hi, Dr Lake,' he said, 'hi, hi.' He waved a hand to all present, before quickly looking at the monitors and the bags of IV fluid. In a low voice he began conferring with the other doctors.

Quickly Josey put through the call to the operating rooms, telling them what to expect. They would transfer their patient there, then, if he survived, he would go on later to the intensive care unit.

Minutes later, she and Guy started on the burr holes. When Dr Cox, the orthopaedic surgeon, came in, Todd and he began to cut off the splints and the padding on the fractured limbs. If necessary they could put in some temporary steel pins to hold the fractures together. The X-ray tech had come in moments before with the films of the fractures he had taken and had hung them up on a lighted wall display unit, beside those of the skull X-rays.

Josey took a deep breath and let it out on a sigh as she glanced quickly at those X-rays, then at the blood-pressure monitor, the pulse rate displayed on a screen, the circulating oxygen level. Then she turned back to Guy and the task in hand. Everything was going as it should, everything was in order. Yet there was no guarantee that their patient would survive...

# CHAPTER TWO

'I KNOW precisely what you're thinking, Josey, and maybe you're wasting your pity. He could be a criminal, a really slimy character,' Brian Todd commented as their patient was finally wheeled out of trauma room one, to be taken to the operating suite on the second floor of the building. They stood, watching him go, surrounded as they were by the usual debris and mess left by the treatment of a serious trauma case.

Josey stood with her hands on her hips until the double doors swung closed behind him and they were left in comparative silence. Only when he was finally gone could she relax somewhat. Again she sighed, turning to look at Todd, also very aware that both Guy and Doug Randall were both still in the room.

'I know all that, Todd,' she said quietly, 'but he's still a human being. He's suffered, he's been in awful pain...and will be for a long time. Doesn't matter what he is, or what he's done as far as we're concerned.'

'Aagh!' Todd made a dismissive sound of near disgust. 'I do my job,' he said, 'to the best of my ability, but probably as soon as we patch up that guy he'll be out on the streets again doing what it is that he habitually does. Maybe a couple of months from now he'll be back with similar injuries.' He began to crash about the room, cleaning up.

'What do you think, Dr Lake?' Josey asked impulsively, goaded by Todd's pragmatism.

Guy, who had been writing up notes in a chart, looked at her. 'It's not our place to judge,' he said. 'That's not

26

part of our mandate. However, I can't pretend that repeat offenders don't present a problem. On the other hand, we have many people who put themselves in harm's way by their lifestyle, or from a lack of common sense—not just those who drink or take drugs. So in the end we can't really discriminate.'

'There should be special surgical clinics for street people,' Todd went on, 'who have problems with drugs and alcohol, so they don't clutter up the regular units.' Todd grinned at her, letting her know that he wasn't as hard as he sounded.

'I don't disagree with that,' she said.

Guy put the cap back on his pen and prepared to leave the room. 'At University Hospital we've been considering a surgical clinic like the one you suggest,' he said as he went out.

'He's nice,' Josey said softly, almost to herself, after Guy had left the room. 'Makes a change from some of the others.'

'Oho!' Todd said. 'Smitten, eh?'

'Not at all,' she said airily. 'Just making an observation, that's all.'

'Oh, yeah! About time you found someone OK. Better work fast, Josey. He'll be going back to University Hospital.'

'Oh, shut up, Toddy.' She flicked a towel at him. 'Would you like to go for a quick coffee-break while we have a breathing space? I can finish up here.'

'Sure,' he said, 'my throat feels like a desert in a drought.'

'When you come back, I'll go for a break.'

Alone in the room, Josey quickly went through the routine of clearing up and setting up for the next case, getting supplies from a back corridor. Any minute now they could be getting another case.

At the end of that corridor, and around a corner, was Alec Ramsay's office. It was in a quiet area where he retreated in rare moments to write up notes and to relax. Josey found herself wondering whether Guy had taken over the same office. Alec Ramsay always left the door open when he wasn't in the room, needing privacy, so that anyone could go in there and get a cup of coffee from his personal coffee-maker, and he always had a big jar of cookies there as well, from which they could help themselves.

Anyway, she decided decisively, she would take a chance and go down there for a cup of coffee. This lull would surely not last long, and she was dizzy from lack of food. After putting in a call to the triage station to say what she was doing, she hurried down the corridor.

The door to the office was wide open and there was no one in the room, although it showed signs of occupancy. Best of all, she could see from the doorway that someone had made coffee in the automatic machine. Tentatively she entered and quickly poured herself a cup of the liquid.

'Josey,' a voice said from the doorway, 'are you all right? You look as white as the proverbial sheet.'

'Oh...' She turned round. 'I...Dr Ramsay usually has an open-door policy for coffee. I, er, hope you don't mind. I'm feeling a bit hypoglycaemic.'

'That's quite all right.' Guy came into the office, seeming to fill the small room with his presence, which wasn't just physical. His cool, appraising glance, not unfriendly, went over her from head to toe, leaving her feeling as though she had been stripped of all defences. 'Help yourself to anything you want.'

'Thank you.'

'Here...' He pulled out a chair. 'Sit down, please.'

'Oh, I can't stay. I've only got a few minutes—seconds, more like it.' She took a convulsive swallow of the coffee, noticing that her lips were trembling. What on earth was the matter with her? Was she so vulnerable and needy that in the presence of the first man she found attractive in a long time she turned into a mental and physical jelly?

'You look awful.' Guy took her arm and made her sit. At her startled expression, he grinned. 'Meant in the nicest possible way, of course.'

'Of course,' she said, trying to inject some sarcasm into her voice. Such solicitude disarmed her in a serious way and to her horror she felt tears pricking her eyes. She had to get out of there fast.

From a small countertop refrigerator he took out a sandwich wrapped in Cellophane. 'Eat that,' he ordered.

'But—'

'No buts. Have you got plenty of sugar in your coffee?'

'I didn't have time to put it in.'

With that, he brought over a jar of brown sugar and a spoon. 'Help yourself,' he said. Then he brought over a large jar of thick cookies and opened it for her. 'Eat at least two of those. That's an order.'

'Thanks.' She smiled, and helped herself to sugar. 'I couldn't wait for Todd to get back.'

'That was quite a case,' Guy said, with a calm understatement that made her smile as he poured himself coffee. 'Especially first thing in the morning.'

'Yes,' she said. 'Do you think he'll make it?'

'Probably. Depends rather on the extent of the brain damage,' he said, 'and whether he has kidney damage. He's reasonably young, so his age is on his side. If he doesn't make it, it won't be for lack of good people to take care of him.'

'Yes.'

'I don't mean just the medical staff. You and Todd were really great in there, for a start,' Guy said. 'I assume that the nurses in the operating rooms and in the ICU are just as good.'

'Yes, they will be. This is a pretty good hospital,' she said, feeling her mood lift with her blood sugar. 'Thank you for the compliment. It isn't often that anyone notices if we're good—they tend to take us for granted, like the furniture. They do notice if we're *not* good, though.'

'That's too bad,' he said.

Josey stood up, hurriedly finishing off the food he had given her. She noticed that on the desk was a wooden plaque, propped up at the back, to which her gaze was drawn because it hadn't been there when Alec Ramsey had used the room.

It looked like something home-made that a child would have made, perhaps as part of a school project. Words were burnt into the wood, laboriously spelled out, it seemed, at once crude, homely and artistic, with that careless artistry of the child. They said, PRIMUM EST NON NOCERE. Josey recognized them as the dictum related to the Hippocratic oath for doctors. 'First of all, do no harm.' Perhaps Guy had children and one had given him that for a birthday present. Those words, on the desk of this very adult, very competent doctor, seemed oddly touching to Josey.

'All right?' Guy said. 'I promised Mac I'd keep an eye on you.'

She swallowed, feeling her colour rising. 'Yes, thank you, much better. I have to go. I...I was just looking at that plaque,' she said. 'Um, it's an admirable sentiment, I've always thought.'

'Yes,' he said pensively. 'It's not always easy to do no harm.' There were nuances in his tone, it seemed to her, that made her alert to other less obvious meanings.

'No,' she agreed. 'We're hampered by the extent of our knowledge—the limitations of it. We're not always aware of the limitations of our competence.'

'It comes back to, "Know thyself",' he said.

'Well...thank you for the sustenance, Dr Lake,' she said formally, making her exit. 'Must get back.'

'See you later, Josey,' he murmured.

As she ran back along the corridor she thought of Joe, his image triggered by those few words she had exchanged with Guy. Joe had been good at his job, among the top few of his class, but also arrogant. Certainly he hadn't possessed that necessary touch of humility, that bit of introspection that enabled you to stand outside yourself and for a moment or two see yourself as you really were. At first she had mistaken that arrogance for self-confidence, had admired it...

As for harm... She thought about that. Harm had been done to her, very definitely. And it would be a long time before she got over it. As surely as she had scars on her body from the operation that she'd had, so she had scars on her psyche. It was almost as though this doctor, Guy Lake, knew about her, this man she had never seen before today. There had been a certain sense of *simpatico*. But that wasn't possible.

As she pulled open the door to trauma room one she knew that she had begun to hope again. And with her it was probably a false hope, because she was flawed as a woman. Who would want her now? Particularly not a man like Guy. Chance would be a fine thing, she thought bitterly.

'Here I am, Todd,' she said breathlessly as she went back into the trauma room, hiding her sorrow well, as she had done for a long time now. 'I had coffee in Alec Ramsay's office. Couldn't wait for you to get back.'

'Just as well,' Todd said, bustling about. 'We've got a guy coming in who had his long hair caught in some machinery he was operating in a workshop. Got his scalp ripped right back.'

'Eek!' Josey said, in mock horror, rolling her eyes, snapping back quickly into work mode. 'There never fails to be something that really turns me off. And I suppose we have to put it back together again?'

'Right in one,' Todd said. 'At least, this will be slow and laborious. A bit of a break, you might say. Apparently he can't go straight to the OR because they have no one free to do it right away, so Dr Lake OK'd it to be done here.'

'It won't be a break for me, Todd,' she said. 'I can just picture it right now.'

'There must be regulations about workers with long hair operating machinery,' Todd said in a disgusted tone.

'There are,' Josey said, helping him get ready. 'Some employers just don't care enough about safety.'

'Yeah. Maybe now some sleazy guy will have to face up to it.'

'Which of the docs is going to do it?' Josey asked. 'It's not quite in Dr Lake's league.'

'Doug Randall will do it, but I guess Dr Lake will want to take a look-see first, and maybe stand by a good deal of the time,' Todd said. 'Anyway, the unfortunate guy's name is Jason Laverne, and he's twenty-five years old.'

Josey felt disappointment that Guy wouldn't be dealing directly with this case, but no doubt more serious cases, such as road traffic accidents, would be coming into the other two trauma rooms while they were dealing with the patient with the ripped scalp.

Don't get involved, she told herself sternly as she went

about her business quickly and efficiently. That was the last thing she wanted...

'Do you want to scrub for this, Josey?' Todd asked.

'Yes, I'll start, if you like,' she agreed, feeling glad that she'd eaten. Lunch, as usual, would be very late.

Guy put his head around the door. 'Give me a shout, Josey, when this patient comes in,' he said, 'so that I can take a quick look. I'll be in one of the other rooms.'

'All right, Dr Lake,' she said, her heart lifting.

'Guy...please,' he said.

'All right, Guy.'

In spite of her good intentions, Josey found herself dwelling on the tentative glimmerings of renewed longings that the new doctor was arousing in her. Better to nip any such attraction in the bud, she told herself, rather than having to deal with frustrated longings at a later date. Contradictory emotions seemed to be pulling her in several directions at once. The sooner she got stuck into work the better.

There was a lot of blood, the scalp being well supplied with blood vessels, and a lot of swelling and bruising of the face. Thick pressure dressings had been applied to the head of their patient by the ambulance crew, through which blood was oozing.

'Will my hair grow back?' Jason Laverne managed to mumble to Josey through swollen, blood-encrusted lips as she stood next to him as he lay on the operating table. His eyelids were so swollen that he could barely see. Obviously he had been well sedated against pain, yet he struggled to articulate his anxiety. 'Is my...is my face all right?'

Josey bent down close to him so that she could catch the slurred words, feeling desperately sorry for him. Even with the bruising and swelling she could see that he was normally a good-looking young man. 'Yes,' she reassured him, seeing that the skin of his forehead was intact, 'the hair will grow back. We'll stitch everything down again, don't worry. Your face is very swollen, but intact. We're going to give you a general anaesthetic and we're getting a plastic surgeon to work on you. I'm one of the nurses. You're going to be all right.'

Josey had on her sterile gown and gloves and her table of instruments ready. In moments Doug Randall would be joining her to make a start, and an anaesthesia staff man was there to give the anaesthetic.

Guy came in, tying on a face mask, just as Doug came in with dripping arms from the scrub sinks, then several things started to happen at the same time. Gently Guy spoke to Jason Laverne about what they intended to do. Within minutes the anesthetist had injected drugs into the intravenous line to render the patient unconscious and had, with Todd's help, intubated him and hooked up the anaesthetic gas lines.

'Now the moment of truth,' Guy said, having come to stand beside Josey. 'Take off the dressings, please, Todd. Let's see the worst of the damage. I may scrub in for a while to help Doug, if this looks as horrendous as I think it might.'

'Right,' Todd said, as he made a start to cut off the swathes of dressings. 'What a mess. I reckon this guy will get his hair cut after this.'

'Keep the pressure on, Todd,' Guy said, 'until we can get it cleaned up. We don't want him to lose more blood than he's lost already. This looks pretty bad, Doug—I'm going to give you a hand. Make a start cleaning him up with the saline.'

'This is the first time I've seen a case like this,' Doug commented soberly as he started to clean the scalp wounds with long forceps holding a gauze sponge dipped in sterile saline, his tone indicating that he was as moved as they all were by this mutilation before them which they had to do their best to reverse. 'Keep the pressure on the top of the scalp there, Todd.'

'We'll need a lot of the fine catgut sutures,' Guy said, standing next to Josey, watching for a moment, 'and the fine black linen thread for the skin. And we'll need lots of wound drains, Todd.' With that, he went out to scrub.

Josey passed sterile drapes to Doug and the operation got under way. Painstakingly they would stop the copious bleeding by either cauterizing the many bleeding vessels or tying them off with pieces of catgut, then they would start on the task of stitching the scalp back so that Jason Laverne would have the minimum amount of disfigurement.

When Guy came to stand next to Josey, gowned and gloved, she was intensely aware of him, a feeling that had for a long time become so unfamiliar that she had thought she wouldn't experience it again. Glancing sideways at him, she took in his appearance—the dark hair that curled up slightly at the back under the green surgical cap that he wore, the well-shaped curve of his eyebrows, his perceptive eyes that met her glance briefly above the surgical mask. Not able to move away, she looked down at her table of instruments and tried hard to concentrate completely on her job.

Two and a half hours later Jason Laverne was in the recovery area of the ER surgical unit. A plastic surgeon, Dr Isaac's, had taken over from Guy part way through the operation to do the more intricate work of stitching back the forehead skin along the hairline, doing very fine work to minimize scarring. Now that it was finished, he, Josey and the anaesthetist settled their patient in the recovery area.

'The operation's over, Mr Laverne,' Josey said, speaking into the patient's ear. 'Can you hear me? Everything's going well. You're in the recovery room now.'

Jason Laverne opened watery eyes, the lids still grossly swollen. Slowly he nodded. With a reassuring squeeze to his shoulder, Josey left the recovery area. Her duty to him was over now, and other nurses would take on his care.

The remainder of the working day went by very quickly. Lunch was a late, snatched snack in the coffee-room, then, hardly before Josey knew it, the evening staff were there for the late shift and it was time for her to go home. Only then did she relax a little and realize how exhausted she was. Thank God it was Thursday and not Monday. Only one more working day and she would be off again for the weekend.

As she and Todd restocked their room after their last case, before getting ready to go home, Josey heard the telephone shrilling down the corridor in Alec Ramsay's office as she was getting supplies out of a cupboard. The ringing went on and on, so she ran down the corridor to answer it.

'Is Dr Lake there?' a breathless young voice enquired before she had a chance to say who she was. 'It's very urgent.'

'He's in the middle of an operation,' she said, knowing that he was still suturing a patient in another room. 'I'm Josey Lincoln, one of the registered nurses. I can give him a message.'

There was a hesitation. 'Tell him it's Rachel. I want him to call back right away,' the voice said imperiously, anxiously. 'Tell him Tom's gone off again, this afternoon. I'm at home, so tell him, please, please, call. And, please, tell him that Mrs Canning has gone home and I can't contact her.'

'Right, I've got that,' Josey said, quickly making a few notes, 'I'll tell him immediately.'

'Thanks.'

Not wanting to go into a crowded room to speak to Guy with what was a very personal message, Josey wrote it down on a piece of paper.

In trauma room two they were engaged in treating a cyclist who had been sideswiped by a truck on a city street and had received multiple injuries. As Josey went in she could see that they were near completion.

'Excuse me Dr Lake,' she said, 'there's a message for you.' As he was gowned and gloved, she held the piece of paper so that he could read her message.

'Josey,' he said quietly, his voice tired, 'would you mind calling back and telling Rachel I'll call in about twenty minutes and should be home within the hour. Tell her not to go out.' His eyes met Josey's for a brief moment as he reeled off a phone number, and she was shocked by the bleakness in his glance. 'That's my daughter.'

'I'll do it now,' she said quietly.

As she hurried out to the corridor to make the call, she contemplated the reality that Guy had a child, that he was married. Maybe it was just as well, she thought. Even so, she experienced an odd feeling of disappointment, of frustrated hope, as though something which could have been sweet had ended before it had had a chance to begin. At the same time she knew that she had been getting ahead of herself emotionally, dreaming about something that might not have been possible. She would have been getting involved with him under false pretences, when he knew nothing about her past. Yet she could have sworn that he was interested in her. She had enough of a normal instinct left in her to be able to pick up the vibes...

# CHAPTER THREE

FORTUNATELY Josey didn't have long to wait for a streetcar on the corner not far from the entrance to the emergency department. One came along moments after she arrived. Standing ankle deep in snow, with a bitter wind whipping cruelly around her face, the only part of her body that was uncovered, she watched the cumbersome vehicle approach along the street. Old-fashioned though they were, the street-cars were perfect in this weather. They swished along through the snow on their metal tracks, like battering rams.

In the warm interior Josey settled down into a seat, glad to be able to sit, to rest her aching legs and feet. Idly she went over the events of the day, while thinking ahead to the hot bath she would have, the hot lemon drink with a dash of brandy, then the soup and omelette with sautéed mushrooms she would prepare for her supper. It was al-ready dusk outside and in the window she could see her reflection mirrored back at her against a dim backdrop of softly falling snow.

It had been on a day something like this that she had first met Joe, Dr Joseph Falconer, on his first day of work as a junior doctor, trained in trauma and emergency med-icine, at Gresham General Hospital. Sometimes it was hard for her to believe that it was actually four years ago that she had first set eyes on him. She had been a young thing then, young and confident, happy in her work. Now the adjective that came to her mind was 'naïve'. Yes, she sup-posed she had been that all right. Yet really she had just been willing to share, willing to compromise up to a point, to accommodate the man she loved. Only now, older and more cynical, or perhaps just more realistic, could she see that in her willingness to give, in the expectation that her giving would be reciprocated, she had been naïve. She should have trodden more carefully, she could see that now. He had taken advantage.

Of course, it was easy to see that in retrospect. At the time she couldn't have known that Dr Joe Falconer, so handsome, clever and charming, had been the sort of person who used people...and used them up. Certainly at the end of those two years of living with him she had felt used up, so weary of giving and not getting much, so exhausted mentally and physically. Even now she didn't want to think too clearly about how it had all ended. Because to think about it threatened her fragile self-esteem which she had begun to build up again. Yet her mind drifted inevitably towards those events, as though her meeting with another new doctor, Guy Lake, necessitated a post-mortem on that which was no more.

They had been busy that day, hectic, four years ago. There had been a pile-up on a road on a day in winter, much like this day. Car crash victims had come in one after the other. They had all been so busy, the staff, that she had only dimly been aware of the new doctor as an attractive man as they'd worked together, sometimes side by side. When it was all over, finally, he said to her, 'Is it always like this?'

There was a rueful, boyish look on his face as he ripped off his face mask and disposable cap to reveal tousled black hair. His expressive brown eyes charmed her when he added, 'How about coming for a drink?'

'What, now?' Josey said incredulously. 'It's half past one in the morning!' They had worked a full day shift and half the night as well, because there had been so much to do

that there was no way that all the staff on the day shift
could leave at half past three in the afternoon when the
shift officially ended.

'I know an all-night bar,' he said, smiling. 'Several, in
fact. The best one is within walking distance. Then I'll
drive you home, if you'll trust me after the carnage that
we've seen today.'

It took her only a few seconds to make up her mind,
mainly because she had a day off the next day. 'All right,'
she agreed, glad to get out of the hospital at last, not to be
alone for the journey home on the snowy streets, haunted
as she was by all that she had witnessed that day. 'Give
me twenty minutes to change.'

In the locker room she had a shower, then dressed in her
outdoor things and met him outside. There was no way of
knowing where it would lead. In retrospect again, it seemed
that from that moment he had set out to charm and seduce
her, although she hadn't known why—she had always
thought of herself as very ordinary, whereas Dr Joe
Falconer had been one of the bright hopes of the hospital,
so she had heard. She had known she had a good brain, the
capacity to work very hard, that she had been good at her
job and had had a flair for creativity in certain aspects of
her life. Beyond that, she'd thought of herself as ordinarily
attractive, nothing special. Men had always warmed to her,
it had seemed, yet she had assumed then that most young
women had the gift to attract. In short, she had been down-
to-earth, matter-of-fact, without an over-inflated ego.

Joe took her to the roof bar of a sophisticated high-rise
hotel downtown which was open until 4 a.m. 'Let me get
you a cocktail,' he offered, 'something exotic after this
pretty awful day.'

All Josey could think of was a Martini. An image came
to her mind of 1940s movie stars sipping cocktails from

triangular glasses behind a screen of cigarette smoke—
Bette Davis, Joan Crawford and Rita Hayworth. The image
made her smile. 'I don't know any exotic cocktails,' she
admitted. 'Perhaps you or the barman could choose one for
me.' Feeling herself to be in a fantasy was a welcome relief
after the raw reality of the day, and she fell into it willingly.

'I know just the thing for you,' he said, leaning over her
in their dark corner which overlooked the panorama of
lights that was the city below them. 'A Mai Tai.'

'Sounds good.' She smiled up at him, feeling the awful
tension of the day receding so that her world was encom-
passed by the dim room where soft music played in the
background. On a tiny circular dance floor in the middle of
the room a couple was dancing. The contrast between this
and the hospital setting was so glaring that she was rather
absurdly grateful to Joe for suggesting it.

The Mai Tai was wonderful. It somehow got rid of the
lingering odours of antiseptics and anaesthetic gases that
permeated the membranes of one's nostrils after a day of
inhaling them. Then there was the scent of perfumed can-
dles, musky and mysterious.

When Joe pulled her up to dance with him she didn't
resist. They clung together, scarcely moving on the circle
of marble that was the dance floor, unselfconscious in the
soft light. She felt that he needed her as much as she needed
him; as much as she appreciated his warm body pressed
closely to hers, he also gained pleasure and reassurance
from her. The knowledge gave her a heady feeling of power
and humility mixed together. It didn't seem to matter that
they had only just met that day. The work they had shared
seemed to encompass a lifetime of knowing, a shared history.

When they left the bar they were the only ones in the
elevator going down from the roof bar, on the twenty-third

floor, to ground level, so that when Joe pulled her into his arms and kissed her, once again she didn't resist. He stopped the elevator on the tenth floor so that they could get out and he could take her into his arms in the darkened corridor where no one walked at that time of night. For a long time they remained locked in each other's arms, as much a reaction against the horrendous day, she could see now, as a powerful physical attraction which had appeared to be mutual.

'Josey, Josey.' He had murmured her name over and over again. 'Will you come home with me?'

As muzzy as she had felt from extreme fatigue and the effects of the alcohol, she had immediately come back to a common-sense reality.

'As much as I would like to,' she'd said, standing in the circle of his arms, his face inches from hers, 'not this time. It's too soon.'

'I'll take you home,' he'd said. Josey had been able to tell from the tone of his voice, from the possessive way he'd kept an arm around her waist, that he'd taken her words as a promise, a postponement only.

After that, it didn't take long for Josey to fall in love with Joe. Six months later she moved in with him at his invitation, into his apartment which he owned, into his life…a life that swallowed up her own, that drew her into his orbit. At the time she had felt flattered and somewhat overwhelmed, although now she couldn't really see why she should have been, except that he was a very good doctor and an attractive man.

She had been proud and happy to be seen with him in public, at hospital dances and parties. Gradually he had taken all that she'd had to offer, had bled her dry, had taken her energy so that she'd had nothing left over for herself as an individual. She had cooked for him and his friends, shopped for food, planned parties which had at first included her own friends and colleagues. Then very gradually, in subtle ways, he had made her friends feel unwelcome, had isolated her somehow in his world. Only her job, her career, had been hers, although even in that he had made her feel that it hadn't been good enough to be a registered nurse, she should have been a doctor...

The streetcar slowed to a halt on a corner and Josey realized that her stop had already arrived. Outside on the snowy street, huddled in her warm coat, she welcomed the cold air on her face—it seemed to blow away the past.

As she walked down the quiet side street towards the small house she shared with two friends, a couple, Donna and Mike, she had the unusual feeling, almost like a prophecy, that with the advent of a new doctor in her department she was somehow expunging Dr Joe Falconer from the position of prominence he had occupied in her mind and emotions for so long. She couldn't have said why it should be so, and there was a fear that she was forming an inappropriate interest in Guy Lake, which could prove to be as wrong as the one she'd had in Joe. No, she told herself emphatically, I will not make the same mistake twice. Anyway, he's married. And she couldn't say that he had really shown any interest in her, he had just been kind.

'Hey, Josey!' Donna, her house-mate, laden with plastic shopping bags, was there behind her, trudging through the snow which was inches deep on the sidewalk. 'How are you? Haven't seen you for at least a week.'

'Hi, Donna.' Josey smiled at her. 'I was sick for a week. This is my first day back to work.'

'Sick? And you didn't let us know.' Donna came up to her, huffing from the load she was carrying.

'I was fine after a few days,' Josey said, making light of

it. 'It was just a matter of staying in bed and drinking lots of fluid.'

'I could at least have made you some soup,' Donna said, as they continued to the front door of the little red brick house with the cedar tree in the small front garden.

The house, once a family home, was divided into two flats—she had the upper one which had one bedroom. They were buying the house together as owners-in-common, she, Donna and Mike. They had been there for eighteen months, ever since she had left Joe, and the arrangement was as perfect as affairs ever could be between human beings.

They shared a common entrance hall, but Josey had her own front door inside that led up to the second floor and her self-contained flat.

'Bye, Donna,' Josey said as they parted. 'Say hello to Mike from me.'

'OK. Don't you be sick again without telling me,' Donna said. She was a nurse in the intensive care unit at University Hospital.

Josey climbed the stairs to her flat, welcoming the cosy warmth of it. Felix, the black stray cat who had seemed to go with the place when they had moved in, stood at the top of the stairs and stretched, murmuring a welcome to her. 'Missed me?' she asked, gathering the cat into her arms. 'I've sure missed you. Let's get something to eat, eh?'

This was her sanctuary, a place all her own, where Joe had never been. Out of her own hard-earned money she was paying a mortgage, her parents having contributed to the down-payment. This place had helped her, was helping her, to regain her self-esteem, her confidence. She was on the hard road back to reclaim the self she had given over to someone else in an insidious process to which she had been largely blind until the effects of it had come home to her in a startling fashion. Still she didn't fully understand why things had happened the way they had, except that she had been young and inexperienced, had taken on more than she had known how to cope with.

In bed later that night, with Felix beside her, after a good meal, Josey mulled over obsessively the last days and weeks she had spent with Joe. It wasn't easy to pinpoint the time when their relationship had begun to deteriorate. Subtle at first, she had sensed a withdrawal in him, and a growing fear in her that her own life had been losing meaning. Perhaps he had been reacting to a necessary desperate withdrawal in her, an act of self-preservation. There had been no question of marriage, and as time had gone by she hadn't thought of it as desirable either.

The beginning of the real end had come on the evening when she had begun to get the pains. 'Joe...' They had been lying in the large double bed, side by side. 'I've got this awful abdominal pain...I've had it for a while.'

'How long?' His voice had been crisp, almost business-like.

She calculated carefully. 'About three hours. I feel a little sick, nauseated. It's mostly on the right side. Maybe it's acute appendicitis.'

'Maybe, maybe not,' he said. Then he pressed his fingers over her abdomen, digging in here and there. 'Does that hurt?'

'Ouch! Yes. There...and there.'

'We'll wait a bit, see how you feel in an hour,' he said. There was annoyance in his tone, an impatience. Amazingly he fell asleep almost immediately after that, while she lay awake, staring up at the ceiling. About half an hour later she went into the bathroom to vomit. The pain was worse and she knew she had to do something immediately.

Joe drove her to the hospital, of course. He did it in an automatic way, as a duty. In her pain and anxiety it was glaringly obvious that he lacked that empathetic personal touch which should have been there between a man and a woman who loved each other. Obviously, her being sick wasn't in the script of the role Joe seemed to have written for her from the beginning in his relationship with her. As she sat in the car beside him, her physical pain and acute anxiety bringing a certain clarity to their interaction, she had to face what was lacking.

It wasn't acute appendicitis but a ruptured ovarian cyst, a surgical emergency that had to be operated on right away.

After the operation, when the anaesthetic had worn off, the surgeon came to talk to her. 'Both ovaries had cysts on them,' he explained. 'Of the one that was ruptured, I had to remove a fair amount of ovarian tissue. On the other ovary, I removed a part that looked as though it was about to rupture.'

Josey looked at him, the fear showing, no doubt, in her eyes, because before she could formulate any words about her future fertility, he said gently, 'I don't think this should make a big difference to your ability to conceive. You still have a fair amount of ovarian tissue there. Of course, your body will take time to adjust, to get over this surgical trauma. There will most likely be some hormonal upset for a while. Just give it time.'

She closed her eyes, feeling weak tears squeezing out from under the lids. 'What about possible future cysts?' She whispered the words. At the same time she felt a very sober certainty that she wouldn't be having children with Dr Joe Falconer...and not just because she had reduced ovaries.

The gynaecologist stood up beside her hospital bed and squeezed her shoulder kindly. 'Most women have small cysts on their ovaries,' he said, 'and don't know they have

them. We know this because we see them when we're looking for other things. Only occasionally does one grow large
and rupture. Some women, as you'll know if you've
worked in the operating rooms, get cysts the size of a foot-
ball, and they say they never knew they had them until they
got symptoms. They just think they're putting on a bit of
weight around the middle. The chances of this happening
again with you aren't great.'

'Thank you,' she whispered.

Those few days in the hospital gave Josey the break she
needed to face up to the fact that all was not well between
her and Joe—the relationship had come to an impasse. You
got to a point, she realized, where you either married a man,
or at least declared a mutual intention to remain together
permanently, or you split up. There didn't seem to be any
middle ground.

Back at home things dragged on for a while, with Joe
working longer and longer hours while she recuperated,
then he talked to her one weekend, the last they spent together. The gist of what he had to say was that he didn't
want to be with a woman who might not be able to have
children. Although he was far from ready to start a family,
he told her, he did eventually want children when he was
more established in his career.

'But not with me?' she said.

'It looks like a big question mark, Josey, a big if. I don't
want to get into that scene,' he said, as though they could
be talking about someone else, a patient perhaps, not about
her.

Not one to procrastinate when faced with the inevitable,
she said, 'You've made everything quite clear, Joe. I'll
move out this week. When I first moved in here I was under
the impression that you loved me. I can see now that I was
a convenience. It was all temporary for you, wasn't it?'

He didn't answer that question. 'Josey, you don't have to be hasty,' he protested feebly, not asking her to stay.

'For once I do have to,' she countered.

The next day she moved out, got friends to help her to move, took an apartment that she could rent by the month while she was hunting for a house. More than anything she wanted a sense of permanence in her life, even if that was ultimately illusory. She wanted a place of her own, where she could cook her own meals, lead her own life, get in touch with the inner peace that she knew was there some-where.

As she finally drifted into sleep she thought about the message that she had taken for Guy from his daughter, Rachel—something about Tom having disappeared again. Who, she wondered, was Tom?

# CHAPTER FOUR

'WE'RE together again, Josey.' Toddy greeted her with those words the next morning when she appeared in the coffee-room of the department early. 'Working in trauma room one.'

'Great!' she said. 'That's what I like to hear first thing in the morning. Mac put me there yesterday because she thought it wouldn't be as bad as general medical emergency, but I'm not so sure about that, considering the day we had yesterday.'

'Well, you've got the weekend to recuperate,' Todd said, moving aside from the coffee-urn so that she could pour herself coffee. 'What would we do, eh, if we didn't have this morning ritual?'

'We'd find something else, I guess. We'd find some other congregation point,' she said.

'Talking of congregation, there's the departmental party in two weeks' time, on the Saturday. It's going to be at a penthouse apartment belonging to the head guy at St Luke's. Are you going to come, Josey? I expect I'll go. It should be a real hoot. You know, you get a chance to see who's separated or divorced and taken up with their secretary, or whatever.' He was referring to the party that took place every two years for the medical and nursing staff from all the teaching hospital emergency departments of the downtown core of Gresham.

'You're a gossip, Todd,' Josey teased. On two occasions she had been to those parties with Joe, as his partner.

'Not a gossip, Josey,' Todd protested. 'I don't generally

pass on what I learn, except maybe to a few trusted people like you. There is a difference, you know.'

'Hmm,' she said doubtfully.

'You haven't said you'll come,' he said, looking at her shrewdly. 'You can come with me, if you like. We can go in a small group.' Todd knew all about Joe, because Josey had eventually told him what he hadn't been able to observe for himself at the time. 'I'll stand between you and any trouble.'

'Thanks,' she said, smiling. 'This is the first I've heard about it, so let me think about it for a while. I don't want to run into Joe Falconer.' Josey kept her voice down as they moved away from the coffee-urn to let others in.

'He's working at St Luke's, so I've heard,' Todd said.

'I try not to hear about him, if I can help it,' she said.

'Maybe that would be the best thing, for you to run into him,' Todd said, 'then you would realize that that louse doesn't mean a thing to you any more.'

'You may be right,' she said thoughtfully. 'But I'm scared.'

'One day he'll be fat and bald, and you'll run into him in a store while he's buying toilet paper and wonder what you ever saw in him,' Todd said.

'Maybe by that time I'll be fat, too…and if not bald, maybe I'll have a double chin and dyed hair, and hopefully he wouldn't recognize me anyway,' she said.

'He'll deteriorate first, Josey, I can tell.'

Quickly Josey drank her coffee and left the room, leaving Todd talking to someone else. She wanted to make an early start. Work was a distraction which she felt she needed this morning, after rehashing the events of her break-up last night. There was more to life than broken affairs. Hashing over them was a self-indulgence that she was trying to put behind her so she could move on.

'Steady, Josey,' a masculine voice admonished her mildly as she came up hard against an immovable object in the doorway as she was going out, while the scent of a subtle, musky cologne filled her nostrils.

'Oh—sorry, Dr Lake,' she muttered, startled by the feel of his warm hands on her bare upper arms as he steadied her.

'I wanted to see you,' Guy said, looking into her face, 'to say thank you for passing on that message yesterday and then making the phone call for me. I appreciated it.'

'That's all right,' she said, feeling a sense of loss as he dropped his hands from her. 'I...I hope it wasn't bad news.' I must be in a bad way, she thought, wanting a man to touch me, even for a moment. No, it wasn't just any touch—it was a loving touch, something she had missed, had longed for but not received.

'No, not exactly,' he said. 'Not something I haven't coped with before.' It was then that she noticed how tired he looked, as though he had had very little sleep. Yet that tiredness did not detract in any way from his masculine attractiveness, Josey thought, her glance going over his face, feature by feature, resting finally on his well-shaped, firm-looking lips. She knew she was getting back to normal when she found herself wondering what it would be like to be kissed by him, to be held in his hard embrace, against that very broad masculine chest...

She cleared her throat, feeling a slow flush rising up over her face, as though he could perhaps read what she was thinking. It wouldn't take much perception on his part to do so. 'I'm glad about that,' she said, giving him a small smile.

'I'll tell you about it some time, if you care to listen,' Guy murmured, looking at her intently. 'I have a feeling that you would be a good listener, Josey.'

'Well, I'm flattered by your untested praise,' she said. 'Actually, I do find myself listening more than talking.'

'We're two of a kind, then,' he said. 'Maybe we talk when we've found the right listener. Hmm?' He raised his eyebrows at her, as though he knew more about her than he could possibly know, and more about her needs. Maybe he was just an ordinary, normal, empathetic man, she told herself...a type of man she hadn't been used to for some time.

'I expect that's it,' she agreed, forcing herself to meet his eyes.

'Perhaps we can do each other a mutual service, then,' he said. 'We'll listen to each other.'

'That would be a nice change,' she said, lightly, airily, as though he hadn't made an offer that contrasted so effectively with what Joe had been. 'I might take you up on that.'

A slow, smile transformed the tiredness on his face. 'I want you to,' he said softly. 'Are we working together again today?'

'Yes.'

'Good. See you in there.'

Admonishing herself for feeling absurdly light-hearted, she went to her room and began the equipment check. Smiling to herself, looking forward to working with both Todd and Guy, she had a feeling that this was going to be a good day.

*Primum est non nocere.* Those words came to her again, with the authority of the many centuries that they had behind them, tried and true. They spoke of normalcy, of kindness and thoughtfulness about the welfare of others, about the trust that those who were dependent on others for vital care were forced to place in other people, often people who were strangers to them. It was really a sacred trust, handed to people like her and Dr Guy Lake. A pity that Joe hadn't extended that dictum to his private life... Sometimes one couldn't help hurting others, but there were ways and means of doing it.

When the telephone buzzed, she was ready for it. 'Several burns cases, coming in by helicopter, should be here in about twenty minutes,' the triage nurse informed her. 'There was a fire in a tyre factory north of the city. Second- and third-degree burns to large areas of the body sustained by four employees. Smoke inhalation...the usual stuff. The paramedics have started IV Ringer's lactate, have cut off most of the clothing and put wet sheets over the burns. It's difficult to treat those things in this freezing weather. Usually they put ice bags on the burns. You'll need more Ringer's, and some IV dextrose in water. Be prepared to intubate. We've got a couple of staff anaesthetists on the way. OK?'

'Yes. I'll be ready,' Josey said. As she hung up she was thinking ahead to what she would need. There would be severe pain and a serious loss of fluid, which would have to be addressed immediately. The paramedics would have got the ball rolling. The thickness of the burned area would indicate the amount of fluid to be replaced in a hurry. A sudden and severe loss of fluid, she knew, could lead to kidney failure.

Todd burst into the room as she was hanging up the last of several bags of IV fluid. 'What's up, kid?' he asked.

Josey told him.

'Spit!' he said. 'I haven't done burns for a while.'

'Not to worry,' she said calmly, 'all the stuff is on hand. Is Dr Lake on his way?'

'Dunno. I'll put a call through to the coffee-room.'

When a staff anaesthetist came into the room, closely followed by Guy, they were ready.

Guy surveyed the room silently as he tied on a face mask and put on a long plastic apron. 'I see that you have absolutely everything ready,' he said, when he had done a quick tour.

'This is the A team,' Todd said, bustling about, checking and rechecking.

'I figured that,' Guy said with a smile in his voice, his glance resting on Josey, so that she felt absurdly pleased, her heart beating fast. For God's sake... She began the familiar internal dialogue with herself that centred on not getting involved—not getting involved under false pretences—a voice that at the same time she tried to silence as she concentrated on work.

'We could possibly need a tracheostomy tray,' he said to Josey. 'If our patient has inhaled toxic gases from burning plastics or rubber or whatever, he could be having respiratory difficulties, in which case we'll do the trach.'

'Right,' Josey said. 'We have one in the room.' She visualized the procedure. Yes, everything was on hand.

'I'll want blood gases done right away,' the anaesthetist said to Josey. 'We could be looking at carbon monoxide poisoning here.'

A call came through from the front desk to say that the first helicopter had landed, with two patients, that they would be getting one in their room.

'All systems go, team,' Todd said. Both he and Josey moved to swing open the doors. The patient would come down in an elevator from the helipad on the roof of the building they were in. It wouldn't take long.

They heard the elevator doors opening and before their patient was far down the corridor they could smell the smoke that clung to him. He was a youngish man, early forties, groaning with pain, even though the paramedics would have given him something for it. Josey and Todd hurried forward to manoeuvre the stretcher down the last part of the corridor and into trauma room one. With all hands helping, they transferred him to the operating table, then removed the layers of blankets to replace them with electric warming pads. As they did this they could see the extent of the burns, third-degree burns, where loose, moist sheet dressings covered the raw, red areas. As well as the odour of smoke, there was the sickly, distinctive smell of burnt flesh.

Having glanced quickly at the preliminary notes the paramedics had made on their patient, Josey saw that his name was John Olivera, so she moved quickly to reassure him and to let him know what they were doing, step by step. With agonized eyes he looked at her. 'We're going to give you a general anaesthetic so that you won't feel anything while we examine you, Mr Olivera,' she said gently.

'We'll do what we can here,' Guy intercepted, 'then we'll probably transfer you to the operating room. We're going to give you lots of fluid to make up for what you've lost from the burns. You're going to be all right.' Guy signalled for Todd to follow him and scrub up.

John Olivera nodded, but didn't speak. He was shivering from shock and cold, disorientated from both the injuries and the narcotic he had received to relieve some of the pain. Josey adjusted heating pads over a covering cotton sheet. They would expose one area at a time to work on him.

Once Mr Olivera had been anaesthetised, Guy and Todd came in from the scrub sinks to put on sterile gowns and gloves. 'We'll do as much of the debridement as we can,' Guy said to Josey, 'then we'll let the plastic surgeons at him. Let's take a look at the torso first.'

'OK,' Josey said as she tied up his gown at the back, then she carefully peeled back the covering on the patient's burnt torso and wheeled the trolley into place beside the table; it contained the sterile instruments and dressings they would need for the debridement.

Josey looked with compassion at the poor man's injuries. She peeled back the temporary dressings so that Todd and Guy could start their sterile procedure. 'When the burnt areas have been cleaned and debrided,' Guy said, 'we'll cover the raw surfaces with moist saline dressings, warmed, which will have to be kept moist constantly. Then the plastic surgeons can get at him in the OR. Now, Todd, give me the small, toothed dissecting forceps to begin with, please!'

'Right,' Todd said. Josey had pushed their equipment into place, and now stood by as the circulating nurse.

'I guess the plastic guys will have to take skin grafts from the back and thighs,' Todd commented as he and Guy made a start. 'He's lucky to have those areas intact.'

'Yes,' Guy agreed.

'At least his face is all right,' Josey commented.

'Yes, I guess he has that to be thankful for,' Guy said, as he bent to the task. 'Irrigate here with the saline, would you, Todd?'

'Right,' Todd said.

After making a check that they had all they needed for now, Josey began filling in forms for the lab.

'Would you get these blood samples to the lab stat, Josey?' Jerry Wong asked, as he handed her the small tubes of blood he had withdrawn from the patient. 'I want the blood gases right away, and a haemoglobin.'

'OK,' Josey said, 'I'll run them along myself.'

'Shall I start the antibiotics right now, Guy?' Jerry asked.

'Yes, please. We'll start with the gentamicin,' Guy said, without looking up. He and Todd were concentrating on their meticulous job. There was bleeding, and Todd was soaking up the blood with pads of gauze.

'Have you got everything you want, Todd?' Josey asked quietly, staring soberly at the sad spectacle in front of her. 'I'm just going to run down to the lab.' She knew that there were two things that could kill a patient with severe burns—shock from loss of fluid, with attendant renal failure, and serious infection from all the dead tissue and contamination of the large areas of exposed raw flesh.

'I'm fine for now,' Todd said. 'I'll need some more gauze sponges in a while. Looks like there's going to be a lot of bleeding.'

The smell of burnt flesh filled the room, overlaid with that of iodine. It was a relief to go out for a few minutes, Josey thought as she walked quickly to the lab with the blood samples. More and more she was admiring the way Guy dealt calmly and competently with each case as it came in, with all the variety, knowing exactly what to do, then just doing it without any jaw-clenching heroics.

Back in the room, she poured more warm, sterile saline for Todd to use to keep the raw areas of flesh moist so that they wouldn't dry out prior to the skin grafts, and more bundles of sterile gauze sponges. It was her job to make sure that everything ran smoothly now that all equipment was on hand.

'Thanks, Josey,' Todd said, looking up and flexing his neck. 'You can give me a shot of IV caffeine as well, if you like.'

'It's your day to fast, Toddy,' she said, smiling.

'When we start on the arms, you can take over from Todd, Josey,' Guy said, looking up at her. 'That way you can both get a break.'

'Great,' Todd said enthusiastically.

Although she tried not to read any personal significance into that simple expedient, the prospect of doing that produced a gamut of contradictory emotions in Josey, the uppermost one being that of anticipated pleasure, the others having to do with the old desire to withdraw. He was married, with children...or maybe he was divorced, with children...whatever. She had to constantly remind herself of that.

'All right,' she said. 'That's a good idea.'

Silence descended on the room as the case continued and Josey filled in the necessary paperwork. Jerry Wong continually checked the patient's vital signs which were displayed on a computerized monitor screen. Josey could see that the blood pressure was a little lower than was optimal, which must be giving concern to him. He was doing what he could to bring it up, with IV fluids and drugs.

Josey sighed. No doubt some of the family members of John Olivera, and the other burns patients, would have gathered anxiously outside in the waiting area of the ER. They must be sick with fear. She could imagine it. Waiting was awful, not being able to see the one you loved.

She wondered how Joe had felt when he had waited for her. Irritation? Impatience? Just going through the motions for the sake of appearances in the place where he worked? Certainly he hadn't behaved towards her as though he loved her. But it was all water under the bridge now.

When John Olivera was finally transferred to the operating rooms an odour of smoke, burnt rubber, clothing and flesh, which even the very effective air filtering system couldn't entirely eliminate while the patient was in the room, still lingered. The case had taken up the first half of the morning.

Todd and Josey dealt with two other minor cases, with Guy and Doug Randall, before Selina Macintosh burst into the room just after twelve. 'Why don't you guys take a lunch-break?' she said. 'Go down to the cafeteria for a

change, one at a time. The other burns patients have all
been moved out, so there's a bit of a lull right now, believe
it or not. Phew! What a smell, eh?'

'Yeah, smells like burning corn stalks down on the farm,'
Todd quipped.

'What would you know about that, city boy?' Mac said.

'Can I go first, Todd?' Josey said. 'I could use a good
nosh.'

'OK, kid, off you go. I'm too keyed up to eat right now,
even though I'm starving,' he said.

Josey took off her soiled protective gear and washed her
hands and arms at the scrub sinks, then put on a clean lab
coat to go to the hospital cafeteria. Most of the time they
didn't get to the cafeteria for lunch, just had a quick sandwich in the coffee-room. This time she was determined to
have a decent meal.

On the way she made a hurried detour to go to the intensive care unit, which was on the same floor as the operating rooms. Since the previous day she had been concerned to know whether the unknown patient had survived.

Once in the unit she went to the office to look up the
man's chart of his medical history, which was both on paper and in a computer. Without knowing his name, she
looked down the racks of charts, which were in alphabetical
order, until she saw John Doe, the name given to someone
whose real name was unknown.

'So he's still alive.' She murmured the words as she
lifted out the chart and flipped through it. There were
mostly lab reports and the nurses' notes, plus some orders
from doctors on the order sheet.

'I see we are of the same mind, Josey,' a voice said
behind her, Guy's voice, as she bent over the chart which
she had placed on the desk in the office.

'Oh...er...' Josey turned round quickly, to see him standing there, his eyes on the chart. 'The unknown man?'

Guy had obviously showered and changed his scrub suit; his hair was still wet, slicked back, and he exuded a pleasant odour of soap. Josey felt her heartbeat quickening, while she thought that even if she had made up her mind to avoid him as much as she could, it wouldn't be possible. So she may as well go with it, sublimate the attraction as much as she could. He nodded, coming to stand beside her to look over her shoulder.

'You smell gorgeous,' she blurted out, the first thing that came into her head. 'Wonderful after that awful smell of smoke this morning.'

He laughed, an action that devastated her emotionally. 'Thank you,' he said, with a little bow. 'I try not to smell like some of my patients. There would soon be complaints.'

This time she laughed. 'Mmm.'

'Looks like they haven't got a name yet for this man,' he said, a lightness in his voice.

'No. I'm glad he made it,' she said. 'I just wanted to take a quick look at him.'

'We'll go together, then,' he said, gathering up the chart. 'I was here last night and he still looked less than pretty.'

'I'll just take a very quick look,' Josey said as she hurried to keep up with him as he strode down the central corridor between the rooms that each housed two patient beds. 'This is my lunch-break, and I'm trying to get to the cafeteria, a very rare event.'

'Great. You can wait for me and I'll join you,' Guy said emphatically. 'I could use some pleasant female company, as well as some food.'

As he walked a little in front of her, Josey looked at him covertly, at the way his body moved under the thin cotton of the scrub suit. There was a manly grace about him that was compelling indeed.

At the bedside Guy went through the chart, while Josey fixed her eyes on the man in the bed, all the time wondering at this doctor's ability to make her face turn pink, as she was sure it appeared now.

John Doe's features were less swollen than they had been in the emergency department, particularly the eyelids, less red and bloody now that they had been cleaned up, yet he had an unhealthy pallor and the bruising was more evident, black and purple. All in all, he looked better than he had on admission. The eyes were closed, the body immobile.

'Is he in a coma?' Josey asked.

'He's in and out of it,' Guy said, looking at lab reports. 'The police come here from time to time, trying to get a name out of him, but no luck so far. He either can't or won't talk, or can't remember. He's definitely sustained some brain damage.' They were talking very quietly.

They didn't linger. In moments they had seen all that they wanted to see, then they took an elevator back to the ground floor of the building and walked to the huge staff cafeteria that served all levels of staff for the hospital, a great meeting-place.

Josey was the first to get a tray of food at the self-service counters and make her way to a table, keeping an eye on a clock so that she didn't overstay her time, not checking to see whether Guy would join her. In fact, she half hoped that he wouldn't, as she was uncharacteristically aware of him and at the moment couldn't think of a word to say.

So when he sat down opposite her, a blankness seemed to descend on her. Quickly she looked up at him, and then down at her food, which she was getting through quickly. He had a salad and a bread roll.

'Weren't you once engaged to Joseph Falconer?' he said, after a few moments.

Of all the things that he might have said to her, that had not been on her list of possibilities. Startled, she looked up at him.

'I know I've seen you with him somewhere,' he went on mildly, looking at her with those astute eyes while he chewed contemplatively on lettuce, a slight frown creasing his forehead between well-shaped dark brows. 'I've been trying to think of where it could have been ever since Mac introduced us yesterday. Was it only yesterday? In this place a day seems like a week sometimes, when we pack so much into it.'

'No,' she managed to say. 'We did live together for a while...two years.'

'That's quite a while,' he said, with no particular inflection in his voice.

'But were never engaged,' she added, perhaps unnecessarily, feeling the need to repudiate Joe. After all, why shouldn't this man know? Her private life was no secret. Yet she felt irritated, as though he had somehow broken through her cover.

'Just as well,' he said, a wry twist to his mouth as he looked at her. 'Marriage often isn't all it's cracked up to be. I must have seen you with him at some hospital function at University Hospital and just assumed...'

'I expect so,' she said tightly, her attraction for him vying with her irritation at his forthright expression of curiosity about her.

'Forgive me if I seem inquisitive. Forgive the intrusion. I know it's none of my business,' he said slowly, quietly, so that none of the surrounding people could possibly hear. 'It's just that I was pretty sure that I had seen you with him at least twice, and... How shall I put this? I never liked him. So now I'm even more curious why a bright, pleasant young woman like you would have been with him.'

The astonishment must have been evident on her face. No one before had said to her that they hadn't liked Joe. They may have thought it, she conceded, but they hadn't said it to her, least of all to him.

'That's a very personal remark, Dr Lake,' she said.

'I know.'

'What...what was it about him you didn't like?' she managed to ask.

'Self-serving is the description that comes to mind,' he said. 'I don't usually talk about my colleagues negatively, but since I hope never to work with him again, I don't suppose a few truths will matter. And I assume you found that out, which is why you are no longer with him.'

'You ask a lot of questions, Dr Lake,' she said, annoyance in her tone. Yet she was perversely piqued at his interest, if that was what it amounted to. There was frustrated hope, too, which was hard to bear.

'It's a bad habit I've got into with patients.' He smiled slightly.

'And you don't know that I'm pleasant,' she said, exasperated.

'True,' he said. 'I like to think that I'm a good judge of character.'

'You know next to nothing about me,' she said, goading him.

'True again,' he agreed patiently. 'But anyone who can work as you do, keep her cool and a sense of humour, do the job well, while remaining agreeable, is in my estimation "pleasant". And I feel that I know something about you, having observed you at social functions with Joe Falconer. I thought then that you were too sweet—as well as beautiful—to be with someone like him.'

'Perhaps you would…er…like to enlarge on what you mean by ''someone like him''?' she said.

'Someone who sees himself as the centre of the universe,' he went on in a conversational tone, as though he were talking about the weather. 'I prefer to talk about you, Josey. Do I flatter myself in your case, about being a good judge of character?'

'I think maybe you do,' she said.

'Perhaps you'll give me a better chance to find out.'

'How?' she said, raising her eyebrows coolly at him, even though her cheeks had that tell-tale flush that she couldn't get rid of just by trying to will it away. 'I assure you I have feet of clay, just like most other people.'

'Will you have dinner with me some time?'

'Um…you're full of surprises, Dr Lake,' she managed to say.

'I suspect that Dr Falconer did very little that was positive for your self-esteem, Josey,' Guy said.

'Why…why should you care?' she said bluntly, trying to challenge him with an astute stare to match his own.

'I've asked myself the same question,' he said quietly. 'I just find that I do.'

Finding herself moved more than she cared to show, she glanced deliberately at one of the very prominent wall clocks that were strategically place in various parts of the cafeteria. 'Right now I'm trying very hard to concentrate on lunch. I don't really want to think about dinner. But thank you, anyway.'

'I'll shut up for a few minutes,' he offered.

'Yes, do,' she said, her face pink again. 'And you're right about Joe. Now that you mention it, I don't like him very much either. So maybe I should be grateful to you for pointing out what a real rat he is.' After cramming the last bit of a bread roll in her mouth, she chewed on it quickly and swallowed.

Then she stood up and lifted up her tray. There was a light of amusement on his face which he seemed to be trying to control. More than anything she wanted to accept his invitation, but common sense told her not to…not yet. Since the break-up with Joe she had been out with other men, of course, but not one of them had meant anything to her. This man, she suspected, would be different, and she was frightened.

'After the experience with him,' she said quietly, looking Guy full in the face, 'it's going to be quite a while before I go out to dinner with another doctor. And another thing, "pleasant" is a rather wishy-washy sort of word. I'm not sure that applies to me, I don't think I want to be "pleasant"—it implies that one could never be anything else.'

Guy met her hectic gaze unflinchingly. Then he smiled, an action that made her heart seem to flip over, perhaps from its rarity. 'Let me know when you're ready, Josey,' he said quietly. 'I think you would be worth waiting for.'

'I don't go out with married men,' she said. With that remark, she turned on her heel and walked out of the cafeteria, placing her tray on the counter at the exit.

And most men want children, she could have added…most men who want to get serious about a woman. She wasn't confident that she could oblige, and the possibility of the deficiency seemed to eat away at her confidence like a corrosive substance. Guy was the sort of man one got serious about, the sort of man one fell in love with. Even going out to dinner with him would be risky on the emotions. Why would he be asking her out if he was married?

Right now she felt that there was no trust left in her. There was a distinct difference between trust and naïvety, she told herself severely as she hurried back to work. Part of growing up was in learning the difference and acting accordingly. Now that she was in her mid-twenties she should know the difference. There was a strong sense that she could trust Guy, but accepting an invitation from him when she had only known him for a day and a half was being naïve, even if he wasn't married. That was the mistake she had made with Joe—getting in too deeply too soon.

She found that her hands were shaking and her heart beating unnaturally fast when she pushed her tousled hair into a disposable paper cap in the ER and took off her lab coat ready for work again.

'Sorry I'm a bit late, Todd,' she said as she walked through the double doors of room one, to find Todd putting the finishing touches to the cleaned room, making sure that everything was in place.

'That's OK,' he said. 'There's actually nothing else booked for this room at the moment, but I'm going to put a call through to the triage nurse to make sure it's really clear, then I'm going to go to the cafeteria for a three-course meal.'

'You'll fall asleep after that, Toddy, from the unaccustomed food intake.' Josey forced herself to be light-hearted, when she really wanted to sound out Todd more about Guy, to confide in him, trusting his down-to-earth opinions which bordered on the cynical. Before she could blurt it all out, Toddy was on the phone to the triage desk, announced the all-clear and was off like a shot.

Josey's emotions were churning because of the unexpected invitation from Guy. She feared being used again, that was why she felt so disturbed, she told herself.

Then there was the other thing. After the operation her body had gradually returned to something like normal, but not normal enough, she thought. The gynaecologist had warned her that it might be so. For weeks she hadn't had a period, then they had started again and she had been very relieved, after a time of feeling sick with anxiety, weighed down with a feeling of dread that she would never have another period. But they had never been regular again.

Never again would she take anything for granted in quite the same way. Like every other healthy young woman, she hadn't thought much about having children. It had been something for the future, something taken entirely for granted, that she would be able to conceive more or less when she wanted to. Now that casualness appalled her.

She hurried out to the side corridor to get more hypodermic syringes from the stock cupboard.

'Hi, Josey. Where have you been hiding?' It was her friend and colleague Linda Sparks, who accosted her out in the corridor. 'I knew you were back at work, but for some reason haven't set eyes on you.'

'Hi, Linda.' Josey smiled at her friend. 'I've been closeted in this room since my return,' she said. 'How are you?'

'Worked off my feet. Can't wait for my holiday in Florida next month. Weren't those burns cases awful? I felt so sorry for those guys. I don't think I've got the smell out of my nose yet,' Linda said chattily while she pulled items out of the cupboard. Josey knew that her slightly offhand manner disguised a deep sense of empathy with her patients. From time to time they were all more than ordinarily sobered by what they had to witness.

They talked hurriedly for a few minutes, catching up on news and gossip. 'What do you think of the new doctor, Josey?' Linda whispered. 'Dishy, eh? And what a hunk! I wouldn't mind getting my hands on that. And he's a great ER doctor, too.'

Out of the corner of her eye, Josey could see Guy coming

towards them down the corridor, no doubt going to his office. 'He's coming,' Josey said.

'Let's meet for lunch or coffee on the weekend,' Linda said quickly. 'Have you got time? We've got some catching up to do. I've heard that Joe Falconer has got himself another live-in woman. Did you know?'

'No, I didn't. I'll call you,' Josey said hurriedly.

As Linda rushed away, her arms full of supplies, she gave Guy a demure smile as he came abreast of them. 'Bye, Josey,' she said.

Josey felt trapped as Guy stopped beside her, a not unpleasant feeling because it was him. 'For your information,' he said quietly, watching while Linda disappeared into trauma room two, 'I'm not married. Because a man has children, it doesn't mean he's married. Does that make a difference to your answer?'

'Well...' she began, swallowing a nervous lump, 'I would have to think about it.' Her eyes focussed on his well-shaped mouth, on the straight nose, the clear-cut angle of his jaw, then the blue-grey eyes that were looking at her with interest.

'I'm not looking for someone to live with me,' he said wryly, 'or someone to marry. Or to have an affair with. So you're quite safe. Just intelligent, pleasant female company once in a while—if you'll forgive the word "pleasant". And if you're thinking I'm a fast worker, Josey, I know how short life is. I also know what I want when I see it.'

Without waiting for a reply, he moved on. By saying what he had, he had somehow made her feel a little gauche, a little prudish, as though she had read too much into a simple invitation...although she didn't think that had been his intention. What she instinctively wanted to do was to run after him and say, Yes, yes, please. But she didn't, of course.

Selina Macintosh came into trauma room one. 'Just popped in to see how you were feeling,' the head nurse said hurriedly, talking fast, 'seeing as yesterday was hectic, not to mention this morning.'

'Tired,' Josey admitted. 'But knowing that I have two days off coming up keeps me going. I'm sure that by Monday I'll be more or less back to normal.'

'Hope so. Sometimes I wonder what normal is myself,' Mac said, glancing around the room. 'What do you think of Dr Lake?'

'He's a great ER doctor,' Josey said immediately, 'and he seems like a nice person, too.' Then Josey remembered the odd, significant look Mac had given her in the coffee-room yesterday morning when she had introduced them. Now she waited for Mac to say something more. The head nurse was nothing if not forthright.

'It was a real coup for us to get him. You two would make a good couple,' she said. 'I thought so when I knew he was coming here. I've known him for quite some time—we've worked together before. He's divorced, in circumstances not of his own making. Mind you, the woman he married wasn't right for him, in my estimation, but I expect he would have stuck it out. He's that sort.'

She was still looking around the room while she spoke, as though taking a mental inventory, before she fixed Josey with a perceptive look. 'I won't say any more, because I don't want to gossip. Just wanted to let you know that he's a great guy, in case you were wondering.'

'I...er...was coming round to thinking that,' Josey said, not knowing what to say, as she had never before been the object of matchmaking.

'Good. He's pretty down these days, and I don't like to see that. He's got problems with his son. Actually, they're not his own kids, they're his ex-wife's kids by a previous marriage.' Mac headed for the door, seeming a little embarrassed that she had said more, having said that she wouldn't. 'Must get on. I don't suppose you'll be idle for long, with this blizzard that's still going.'

'No…' Josey stood for a moment watching the double doors that swung to and fro after the head nurse had departed. It wasn't often that Mac interfered with anyone's private life, although she had offered to be Josey's confessor with regard to Joe. Maybe she had noticed a change in her, was disturbed by it.

When the telephone buzzed she was ready. 'Hello. Room one, Josey Lincoln speaking,' she said. 'Right…right.'

Then she dialled the number of Todd's pager.

'Road traffic accident,' she said when he answered. 'Two cars collided on an icy road. Five people involved in the cars, plus one pedestrian. All coming to us.'

'Beat you to it,' he said, chuckling, 'I'm halfway through dessert and coffee.'

'Finish it, Todd.' She laughed. In a few minutes she would be working with Guy again and she found that she was looking forward to it.

# CHAPTER FIVE

'COULD I give you a ride home?' Those simple words came at the end of a long, exhausting day.

It was five o'clock in the evening and they had just come to the end of a case, when they should have been off duty at half past three. The road traffic accidents had kept on coming in. There was, they heard, still a raging blizzard outside, making visibility on the roads about zero. They didn't know for sure, of course, because there were no windows in the trauma rooms, or in the corridors that were immediately off those rooms. Sometimes Josey thought of herself as a mole, hidden away under the earth.

Guy said those words to her when they were alone in the room that was a shambles after their last case had just been wheeled out to be taken to the operating rooms. Todd and other staff had gone out on various errands, or simply off duty.

Josey nodded, not trusting her voice. So tired, she felt that she could burst into tears.

'I'll meet you outside the ER entrance,' he said. 'In, say, twenty-five minutes?'

Josey nodded again, feeling tears prick her eyes. There was no thought now that she would not accept his invitation, if not for dinner, then for a ride home. The prospect of waiting for a streetcar in a howling gale didn't appeal to her. Sobered by the horrendous things they had dealt with that day, she wanted nothing more than to go to the coffee-room to make a cup of tea, then change to go home.

They were waiting for the hard-pressed nurses on the evening shift to come and relieve them before they could leave.

Guy looked as exhausted as she felt. All that day he had been great to work with. His quiet professionalism had got them through; they had all worked so well as a team.

Two nurses came in, part of the evening shift. 'Here we are, Josey,' one of them said. 'Sorry it's taken so long for us to get to you. It's bedlam out there. Now, where are you at?'

Josey gave a quick report of what there was left to do then, throwing her dirty gloves and face mask into the garbage bag, she left the room without a backward glance. After washing her hands, she marched without looking to right or left to the coffee-room. There was no one in there. It was a relief to boil water in a few moments, pour some over a teabag in a mug as she fought down an uncharacteristic feeling of hysteria. She knew she had come back to work too soon after having had flu—today's exhaustion proved it.

Guy came in as she stood against the sink, sipping her tea, her hands cupped comfortingly around the hot mug. With a perceptive glance at her, he wisely said nothing, but made himself a mug of tea and took it out with him. 'See you in a few minutes,' he said from the doorway.

Josey shot him a quick glance and nodded as he went out.

The first thing that struck her when she went outside was the biting wind then the snowflakes as she emerged from under the portico that surrounded the entrance to the ER. Bundled up in her sheepskin coat, a warm hat pulled down over her ears and a scarf covering the lower part of her face, she felt well insulated against the cold. Nonetheless, it was always a shock when one first emerged into it, and Josey stood leaning into the wind as the snow swirled around her, wondering how Guy would recognize her, or she him. He hadn't told her what type of car he drove.

It was already dark outside, now that she was so late going off duty. The area by the entrance was well lit, and snowflakes sparkled in the light of streetlamps beyond the sheltered area.

No cars were allowed to park in the short, curved driveway under the portico, so that ambulances would have a clear right of way. Visibility was so poor that she could scarcely see the buildings on the opposite side of the street.

'Josey?' She felt a touch on her arm and turned round to see Guy's tall, very masculine figure beside her, swathed in a heavy winter coat, with the collar turned up, his head bare. 'My car's over there.' He indicated the small parking lot that was a few steps away from the department.

It seemed perfectly natural that he should take her arm and escort her through the blizzard to his car, where she saw that he had a reserved parking space. The touch of his gloved hand on her arm gave her that rare feeling of being cosseted and cared for, something she hadn't experienced very often with Joe, she knew now as they struggled against the wind.

'What a day, in more ways than one,' he said, as he unlocked the door and opened it for her and waited while she settled herself in, taking plenty of snow with her.

'Well, where do you live, Josey?' he said, when he was settled beside her, having brushed off snow from the windows of the car.

When she told him, he looked surprised. 'Ah, very close to where I am,' he said.

'I'm glad you won't be going out of your way.' She smiled as she took off her hat and loosened her scarf. Very soon the heat would be blasting away inside the car, cocooning them in an artificial world, while the inhospitable elements of nature raged around them ineffectually. The car was a rugged, all-terrain vehicle, like a Jeep, with large tyres that held the chassis well above the ground and the snow which was thick in those areas that hadn't been cleared by snowploughs.

Guy let the engine run for a few minutes to warm up, before he carefully eased the car out of the parking space and left the parking lot to join the line of traffic crawling along the street. 'Now,' he said, giving her a speculative look, 'I know where you live. Just let's see if I can make it.'

'I have confidence in you,' she said, smiling. 'It's very nice not to have to wait on the street corner, and then maybe not get a seat. I don't own a car, can't afford one.'

The main streets were clearer, having been ploughed. Huge ploughs, with flashing blue lights, and large salting trucks loomed up from time to time ahead of them through the swirling snow. Josey felt herself relax.

A car phone shrilled, breaking into her reverie just after they had turned onto another main street and were heading east towards the area where they both lived.

'Hello?' he answered. 'Hi, Rachel.'

Josey remembered that Rachel was Guy's daughter, the one for whom she had taken and given messages.

'When did he go? And where did he go?' Guy was saying, his words giving Josey a feeling of apprehension. Maybe she should offer to get out at the next main intersection and take the streetcar. She had a premonition that something was up.

'I'll go there,' he said to Rachel. 'You just stay put in case he calls.' When he disconnected he looked grim, gripping the steering-wheel tightly, a serious set to his features.

'Is there a problem?' Josey asked. 'If you have to go

somewhere, I could get the streetcar. You don't have to take me home.'

The man beside her took a deep breath and let it out on a sigh, as though he could dispel his obvious worry, which she couldn't so much see as sense.

'I have a son, fifteen,' he said heavily, keeping his eyes fixed on the road ahead, 'who has a mental health problem that developed recently in the past few months—bipolar disorder. At least, that's the temporary diagnosis—we're not absolutely sure about it at the moment.'

'That's the disorder where people have alternating periods of elation and depression, isn't it?' Josey asked tentatively, looking at Guy, feeling the anxiety that was evident in every line of his body. 'It used to be called manic-depressive psychosis?'

'Yes,' Guy said. 'When he feels depressed he sometimes goes out, mainly to visit someone, usually without their knowledge that he's coming—school friends, normally people he's already been with during the day. Just takes off without telling anyone that he's going, or where he's going. It usually happens after school. It's just that he doesn't let us know, and he sometimes stays out all night, although up to now we've always found out where he's staying for the night. Fortunately he likes his school, has good rapport there with some of the teachers.'

'So he doesn't actually skip school?' Josey asked, wishing there was something she could say or do to lighten Guy's load.

'No, not so far, although while he's there he sometimes gets withdrawn mentally. Usually his teachers let me know pretty quickly,' he said.

'That doesn't sound too different from the usual behaviour of quite a lot of fifteen-year-olds,' Josey ventured, 'especially boys. They can get very stubborn and uncommunicative. Not that I speak from personal experience. I'm thinking of brothers of friends.'

'Yes. It's just that what he does is exaggerated,' Guy said. 'It's as though he thinks that by some magical process we will know where he is. Or maybe he just doesn't think at all. You can imagine what anxiety that causes me and my daughter, especially in weather like this. He wouldn't be the first young guy like that found frozen to death in some back alley.'

'Have you any idea where he might be?' Josey asked, turning in her seat to look at his serious profile. How tired he looked, she thought. At least she could go home and put work out of her mind as far as possible and relax. It sounded as though he wouldn't be able to relax very often.

'Not precisely. Rachel thinks he may have gone to see some school friends in a certain area. The trouble is, if there's no one home, he tends to hole up in their garage, if it's open, or any garage nearby and wait for someone to come home. I've given him a mobile phone, but I've found that when he's in one of the depressed moods he seldom takes it with him.' The words were matter-of-fact, bleak.

'And you have to go to look for him?' she said.

'Got it in one,' he said. 'If I didn't do it, God knows what would happen to him. Rachel and I, and our housekeeper, Mrs Canning, are the only ones who really care about him on a day-to-day basis, apart from a few good friends, and some of his teachers. They can't do much except be there for him when he visits them. They're pretty good in calling us when he shows up. My fear is that one time he won't show up anywhere he's known.'

'Where was your housekeeper?' Josey asked, not sure how far Guy wanted to confide in her.

'She had gone home early because of the weather. She doesn't live in, she lives with her elderly mother,' Guy explained. 'Usually she's really great, let's me know what's happening at all times. I don't know what I'd do without her.'

And where is the boy's mother? she wanted to ask, but didn't. That question seemed to hang in the air, something that couldn't yet be spoken about because they didn't know each other well enough, and no doubt because he didn't know whether she wanted to hear more of his problems, let alone be burdened with them.

'Will you let me come with you, Dr Lake?' she said, making up her mind quickly. 'I'd like to. You must go to look for him before you take me home. It's the weekend tomorrow, I've got plenty of time.'

'I couldn't do that,' he said, turning to glance at her. 'This could take some time. And for heaven's sake call me Guy.'

'I want to come…please, Guy.' she said. All at once she wanted to get to know him better, wanted to understand more about his private life, to know why he had asked her out to dinner when they had only known each other for two days. Her reservations began to seem of lesser importance.

'All right,' he said, on a sigh, 'but if we don't find him quickly, I'm going to take you home.'

'Agreed,' Josey said. 'Tell me more about your son.' The car was warm now, a cosy shell, inducing a certain intimacy.

'His name's Tom. This illness became apparent with depression and slightly odd behaviour. He had to be admitted to a psychiatric hospital for a few days.'

'I don't know much about these types of illnesses,' she said when he paused.

'People with this disorder, as well as schizophrenia, don't respond to talk therapy,' he said. 'Many of them end up homeless, living on the street, because they can't cope

with the simple stresses of ordinary life. A lot of mental
hospital beds have been closed.' There was a controlled
anger and frustration in his voice.

'Yes.'

'My biggest fear is that Tom will disappear into that
underworld and I won't be able to find him, although it's
early days with him... Maybe it will never come to that.'

'Yes, I can understand that, can sympathize with it,' she
murmured.

'It rules my life,' Guy said quietly, almost as though he
were talking to himself, admitting the fact to himself, rather
than trying to elicit any sympathy from her.

'Is he on any medications?'

'Yes, lithium, which works well. But he refuses to take
it some of the time.'

They had driven up some side streets, the car engine
straining a little as they ploughed through deep snow on
some of them that hadn't been cleared. The headlights on
snow emphasized their small, enclosed world, one that was
fraught with anxiety at that moment. 'I'm going to where
some of his friends live,' he explained. 'Rachel is phoning
around to try to find out where he might be. She'll call
back shortly.'

'I see,' Josey said, wanting to reach out and touch him,
to show him that she understood something of this seemingly insurmountable problem. At this point she didn't want
to ask what the long-term prognosis might be for his son.

The telephone rang again when they were in an area just
a few blocks north of where they both lived. Guy talked to
his daughter as they turned down into a small dead-end
street, then took a turn to go into an alley at the back of
some houses, a lane for garages and back entrances to the
gardens of the houses. He brought the car to a halt.

'I'm going to get out and have a look around, Josey.

You stay here, keep an eye out for him, would you? He's about average height, slim with dark hair.'

'All right,' she said.

'I wouldn't be surprised if he's quite inappropriately dressed for the temperature. Several of his friends live on this street, it's not far from the school.' He turned up his collar, buttoned up his coat and put on gloves. 'Rachel phoned Tom's best friend, and the boy isn't home, so maybe he's waiting in a garage, or maybe he's gone to another house. I'll leave the engine running so you can keep the windshield wipers and the lights on.' With that, he got out and slammed the door.

There was an eerie quiet after he had gone, other than the muted swish-swish of the wipers, sounds muffled by the snow. Through the swathe of clear glass left by the wipers, Josey peered out through the blizzard. What an awful thing to have to do, she thought as she watched while Guy progressed down the lane in front of the car in the glow of the headlights. Now he was simply Guy, not Dr Lake; he was simply a responsible man worried almost out of his mind for the safety of his son.

Then she heard him calling, 'Tom! Tom!' Feeling helpless, she could only watch his blurred figure as he waded through snow and then disappeared through a garden gate, no doubt to enquire at the house. Then she watched him work his way up the back lane, going from side to side, where he must know that Tom had friends.

When he had covered the lane ahead of the car, he came back and went to the rear of the parked vehicle, down what remained of the back entrances. Josey peered around her, alternately letting down windows to clear them of snow. There was a wiper on the back window, too, so that she could see something of Guy's progress.

Suddenly one of the rear doors was opened and she

turned round swiftly, her heart pounding, not having seen anyone approach. A boy, wearing a sweater and light trousers, bare-headed, without gloves, stood in the aperture of the open door. There was snow on his hair and on the upper part of his body.

'Tom?' she said.

He didn't answer, simply stared at her, his face expressionless. There was no doubt in her mind that this was Tom.

'Get in, Tom,' she said, 'and close the door, please. Your dad's looking for you.' Although she felt startled and more than a little apprehensive, she forced herself to smile and keep a calm expression on her face, not wanting to frighten him away before Guy could come back.

Without a word the boy clambered into the back, closing the door. He was shivering convulsively, his face blue with cold. Quickly Josey took off her own full-length sheepskin coat and, twisting round in her seat, she offered it to him. 'Put this on, Tom,' she said, trying to put some authority as well as kindness into her tone. 'You must be freezing.'

He didn't look at her but did as he was told, his head hanging down. Water was dripping off strands of hair, down his face. 'Do the buttons up,' she said. Next, she passed him her gloves and hat. 'Put those on, too.' The interior of the car was warm, and she had warm clothes on under her coat.

What to do next? Guy was nowhere in sight now. She pressed the horn three times to get his attention, hoping that not too many residents on the back alley would come out to see what they were doing. She was concerned that Tom would decide to leave the car suddenly. 'Are you all right?' she asked.

Still he didn't speak, just sat hunched forward in her coat, his head hanging down on his chest so that she couldn't see his face.

'Mmm, that was great,' Josey said when she had finished eating. 'I didn't realize how starving I was.'

'We all needed that,' Guy said, wiping his hands on a paper napkin. 'Do you want anything more, Tom?'

'No,' Tom said.

'In that case, it's home,' Guy said. 'Come to my place, Josey, have a mug of hot chocolate. Then I'll take you home. OK?'

'OK,' she said, feeling strangely contented, even with the more or less silent boy in the back seat, an unknown quantity. 'There's nothing I'd like better at this moment.' It was as though she were part of this family for a brief time, included within their orbit. Palpably, Guy cared for this boy very much.

'First of all,' Guy said, picking up his cellphone, 'I'll put through a call to Mrs Canning to ask her if she could come over for a while. She's just over on the next street and she's used to coming over at short notice when I'm on call, if need be.'

He appeared to be as highly organized in his private life, Josey considered as she watched him covertly, as he was in his professional life, without being too obsessional or uptight about it. As organized, that was, as he could be with a son whose behaviour became unpredictable once in a while.

Their home, only two streets away from her own, was in an area that was part old, charming residential and part small shops and cafés on the main street, as well as on a subway line. It had become quietly trendy in recent years, an interesting mix of residents of all ages who seemed to mesh successfully.

Guy got out first, after parking in the street outside the house. With the lamplight glittering on pristine snow, the street was like a silent fairyland. The house was large, old, of mellow red brick, from what she could see of it, with a small garden and trees at the front.

The front door burst open and a girl ran out, to come up to Tom and put an arm round his shoulders. 'Come on,' she said to him. No recriminations, no other comments.

Josey could see a woman standing in the doorway, waiting for them, whom she assumed to be Mrs Canning. As they all walked up the garden path Josey could see that she was a mature woman who appeared to be in her early sixties, with soft, grey, curly hair and an intelligent, kindly face. She was well able to cope, no doubt, with this family.

'And where have you been this time, Tom, as soon as my back was turned, eh?' the woman said, admonishing him at the same time that she put her arms around the boy, who was still enveloped in Josey's coat. 'We've a hot bath waiting for you, so you come up now and get right into it.'

When Tom, accompanied by Rachel, had gone upstairs, the housekeeper addressed Guy. 'I'm sorry that this has happened, Dr Lake,' she said. 'I guess I shouldn't have gone home so early, but he was here, home from school, so I figured he would be all right, that he was here for the evening.'

'Don't you worry,' Guy said. 'It wasn't your fault in any way. You know what he's like. If he's made up his mind to go out he'll just go, regardless.'

'Nonetheless...'

Guy put a hand on the woman's shoulder. 'Meet Josey Lincoln,' he said. 'We work together, and she helped me look for Tom. Josey, this is Mrs Canning.'

'Pleased to meet you,' Mrs Canning said, extending her hand.

In the light and warmth of the front hall, everything seemed decidedly to be returning to normal.

Rachel came back down the stairs, carrying Josey's coat, hat and gloves. 'Tom's in the bath,' she said.

'Rachel, this is Josey.'

'Hi,' the girl said, holding out a hand solemnly for Josey to shake. 'We talked on the phone.'

'Yes. Hello,' Josey said, smiling. Rachel was a short, thin, serious-looking girl, with dark hair and eyes.

'I'd better go up and keep half an eye on him,' Mrs Canning said.

'Come into the kitchen, Josey,' Guy said, sighing, as though a load had been lifted from him, taking her arm and leading her through the hall to the back of the house. 'I'll make hot chocolate for all of us.'

'That sounds like a good idea,' Josey said. There were so many unanswered questions, things that she longed to ask him. All in good time, she told herself. She would wait until he volunteered the information. Or not, as the case might be.

The house looked pleasantly untidy, lived-in, a real home rather than a show house. There was nothing ostentatious about this man or his home...something else that was different between him and Joe. For Joe, so much had hinged on appearances.

When Guy had heated milk for hot chocolate, he took two mugs upstairs, then came back to join Josey. In the few minutes he was away she went into a washroom, then stared at her pale face in the mirror as she was washing her hands, noting how cold and tired she looked, her hair curling around her face in damp tendrils, the vestiges of snow still glittering in it.

'You look like a snow maiden,' Guy said when he handed her a hot drink. 'With snow in your hair.' He was dressed in casual clothes that, nonetheless, hung elegantly on his large frame, clothes of good quality...like the man.

She found herself staring, taking in his appearance avidly, as though she could understand Guy Lake the man, rather than the doctor.

'I feel like one,' she said.

He put down the mug that he had held cupped in his hands and put his hands on her face, warm and comforting. 'Yes, you are cold,' he said very softly. 'Thank you again, Josey. You helped me to get through. All in all, it's been quite a day. I'm sure you didn't suspect you were in for this when you accepted a ride home.'

'No...but I don't mind, really. Mmm, that's nice.' She closed her eyes as the warmth of his hands, hot from holding the mug, penetrated her cold skin. Such small, spontaneous gestures that meant a lot weren't things that Joe had indulged in very often unless they had been a means to a desired end for him, she could see that so clearly now, so she stood there with a feeling of surprise. She had forgotten how nice it was to be singled out for such attention...more than that, to feel worthy of such attention.

'Josey...' Guy murmured her name, then before she had time to realize what he was going to do, he had tilted her face up and was kissing her, his warm, firm mouth covering hers. Involuntarily she stiffened, held herself rigid, then she relaxed because it was the most wonderful sensation she had experienced for a very long time, and she dared not open her eyes in case it wasn't real and she was living in a fantasy.

That feeling didn't last long, for he was very real, this large, very masculine man who was gentle at the same time. Josey opened her eyes a fraction to look at his dark head bent down to her, then let her eyelids flutter shut. His eyes were closed as he kissed her...not like Joe, who was often watchful, to see what effect he was having on the woman he was with, as though he were watching himself perform, rather than being lost in the moment.

'I…I don't think…' she began when they moved apart. Her heart was thudding, bringing heat to her face.

'It's all right,' he murmured. 'It means what you want it to mean, no more, no less. I've wanted to kiss you from the moment I saw you the other day.'

Guy's arms went round her again, easing her against his warm body as he kissed her again, and she put her arms up around his neck and kissed him back, half-surprised at herself yet unable to prevent herself from doing it, the most natural thing in the world. Except that she had only known him for two days…

He lifted his head from hers and kissed her neck, her forehead, her eyelids.

'We've only known each other for two days.' She murmured the feeble protest out loud.

'Is that all?' he said, laughter in his voice. Then he kissed her on the mouth again.

If only this could go on for a long time, if she could fall asleep in his arms like this… Right now she was so tired that she could have fallen asleep on the floor, especially if he was with her.

A door slammed up above them, then footsteps sounded on the stairs. Guy eased away from her, held her at arm's length for a moment as he looked at her with eyes that were alight with a rare warmth, a muted desire. His lips parted in a slight smile, as though he was bemused by his own reaction to her, his own need. Instinctively she knew that he needed her. Less willing to reveal her own feelings, even to herself, she stood with her lips slightly parted, looking dazedly back at him before turning away to pick up her cup. She felt punch-drunk, as though all this were happening in a dream.

Rachel came thumping down the stairs and into the kitchen.

'He's still soaking in the bath,' she announced, in a very mature way.

'That's great,' Guy said, putting an arm round the girl's shoulders and giving her a quick peck on the cheek. 'I'm going to drive Josey home in a few minutes. I won't be long. Will you and Mrs Canning be all right? Tom should sleep now. I'll make sure he's taken his medication before I go.'

'We'll be OK, Dad,' she said, going out again.

'You can see why I'm not looking for someone to live with me,' he said bluntly, while giving her an ironic smile.

'There are worse situations, Guy,' she said. 'Much worse. Although realizing that isn't of much help to you, probably.'

'I know it, but when Tom takes off like that, it doesn't seem that anything could be much worse,' he said. 'I know what the expression ''sick with worry'' means. I've been to see his teachers a few times, they understand the situation. Surprisingly, he's managing to hold his own academically. He's a bright young man.'

'That must be a relief,' she said. 'I guess that this particular episode of depression won't last long?'

'No. He'll be back to normal soon, especially with the help of the medication. It may recur, of course, if he really does have bipolar disorder.'

Josey nodded in commiseration and sipped the hot chocolate, while feeling tremulous with a heightened awareness of him so close to her. It seemed amazing that he had actually kissed her when she had wanted it so much. Once again she was putting herself in a vulnerable situation. Whenever he came within touching distance of her she felt a loss of control, as though she were melting into him.

'When you lived with Joe Falconer, did he get you to cook for him pretty quickly?' Guy asked as he stood leaning against the kitchen counter, casually relaxed now, and when Josey looked up at him, startled, she could see by the light in his eyes that he was teasing her. Now that his son was safe he was actually teasing her! Two days ago she wouldn't have guessed that she could respond to that, could actually see a kind of bitter humour in the situation between her and Joe.

'Well…yes,' she said, meeting his eyes. 'As a matter of fact, he did.'

'And do his laundry?' he persisted.

'Afraid so,' she admitted.

'And make you feel flattered for doing it?'

'Yes.'

They both laughed. Then there was a silence, a slightly awkward, loaded silence, so that Josey had to turn away from him as an atmosphere of intense awareness seemed to spark between them, and her mood changed as some insight into her own past behaviour came to her.

The humour gave way to a poignant sense of lost time, coupled with the memory of rejection when it had become known that she might be less than fully fertile. How could she have given herself so passively to someone who had not been good for her?

'I know I was a pushover,' she mumbled, not looking at him. 'I…I hope I've grown up at least a bit since then.'

Turning sideways to him, she clutched tightly at the mug she was holding, feeling her lips tremble as she took a sip from it.

In a moment Guy was beside her, turning her to face him.

'Josey, I didn't mean to disparage anything that you felt

for him. I'm not trying to make fun of you.' There was an agonized note in his voice.

'I know. I've had a long time to think about it. Just don't make me feel that you're sorry for me, that's all.' Tears that she couldn't control were pricking her eyes. That was what unaccustomed gentleness did for you.

'Sexual attraction, although very important, isn't enough, is it?'

'No.'

'More like staying power, consistency, commitment, mutual respect.'

'Mmm.'

'And simple courtesy and kindness. Our friend Dr Falconer has a lot to answer for, I think. He hasn't done anything positive for your self-esteem. Which is a pity, because you have a lot to be confident about, Josey Lincoln,' he said with uncanny shrewdness, his eyes searching her flushed face, noting the moisture in her eyes.

'I'm trying to stop thinking about him so much,' she said. 'I *was* in love with him. It wasn't just sexual attraction. That's my excuse, my reason. Now I'm asking myself why I got myself into the situation…whether I can trust my own judgement.'

'We all ask ourselves that,' he said.

'I don't know why I'm telling you all this,' Josey muttered. 'This isn't really the time, is it?'

Guy took the cup from her hands and drew her to him. 'I want to know. Look at me,' he whispered. 'My God, I wish I were free to…' He didn't finish the sentence. Instead, he kissed her, a deep, searching kiss that left her weak at the knees, pliant in his arms. She had wishes of her own. Not yet, she told herself, not yet.

'I must go,' Josey said, drawing back, understanding all too well at that moment that he wasn't free, any more than she was free to get involved, even slightly, with a man who didn't know and understand her medical history.

'Yes, of course.' He drew back from her. 'I'm sorry to have kept you so long after such a hectic day. It was selfish of me. Thank you again, Josey, for coming with me. Your being there made it all easier.'

'I'm glad.'

The snow had stopped falling by the time they emerged once again from the house, then in moments he was easing the car away from the kerb. 'You'll have to direct me,' he said. Now that they were alone, the immediate crisis over, something of their professional relationship began to creep back, together with such an acute mutual physical awareness that it seemed almost like a tangible thing in the confines of the car. Josey struggled with these two mutually exclusive urges as she huddled down into her enveloping coat.

It didn't take them long to get to her place, and Guy pulled up in front of the house. They sat looking at each other.

'I feel that a little explanation is in order,' he began. 'You must be rather puzzled by certain things.'

'A little,' she admitted. 'But, please, don't feel obliged to tell me if you would rather not. After all, it's none of my business really.'

'I prefer to clear the air,' he said. 'First of all, I'm divorced. Both Tom and Rachel are my ex-wife's children by a previous marriage…we didn't have any of our own. Tom was always a little difficult to manage. My wife, Beth, took off when Tom was four years old, because she couldn't cope with her own children, didn't want to cope with them, so I kept them, of course. Eventually I got custody of them.'

'I see,' Josey murmured noncommittally, sensing in him

both a muted bitterness and a need to talk, to unburden himself to someone who would keep a confidence, just as she had unburdened herself to Mac when she had been invited to do so. Just speaking the words to a trusted person had been a relief, at a time when she had been in despair and had had the sense that no one else could possibly have understood.

'Beth doesn't want to know about Tom's illness now, she seems to have closed her mind to it. So I've decided not to burden her with it—there would be no point because she isn't going to be a help to any of us. I love them both, of course. The children, that is,' he said. 'As far as I'm concerned, they're my children. To them, I'm their dad. I was twenty-two when I married. Rachel was a tiny baby, and Tom was a bit more than a year old. I guess I felt sorry for them all. I must have been crazy. Idealistic, anyway. Beth was already divorced. So, you see, Josey, you were no more foolish than I was. Less so.'

'Other people do understand, you know, Guy,' she ventured, saying his name tentatively, 'although you feel that it's all so very personal and private, that no one else could possibly know what you're feeling.' She looked down at her gloved hands clasped in her lap. 'I hope that doesn't sound too homespun...'

'No.'

'Do they see their mother?'

'They see her now and then. It's up to them. They can make contact whenever they want, then it's up to their mother to respond or not. Often it's not, because she's frightened by Tom's illness. There's mental illness in her family, you see,' he said, gazing out through the windshield of the car where the lights lit up the road. 'There's a genetic component to this illness, as I expect you know. Anyway, she's living with another man, not married to him.'

'Do you care?' Josey said baldly, turning in her seat to look at him, desperately needing to know. 'Do you still love her?' Not sure how she had the nerve to come out with that now, she was nonetheless determined to cut through to the truth, otherwise they would go round in verbal circles.

'No. No to both questions,' Guy said thoughtfully. 'We married when I was too young. She was older, and I guess I was flattered by her attention…to try to put a handle on it, to make a complex situation simple for the sake of expediency. Also I had a crazy idea that I could look after them, before I was really established in the world. In fact, I'm glad that things have turned out this way from some points of view. But right now I feel I shall never be free… Tom will go on needing me for quite a while, unless someone comes up with a superlative treatment.'

'Perhaps none of us is really free, we each have a past. I know it's never simple,' she said. What would he think of her dilemma? That it was very possible that she could never have children, or at least might find conception difficult? The need to know that she could have a child took on a greater poignancy as time went by, it was on her mind most of the time.

'You know, Josey,' he went on quietly, as though musing to himself, 'in an odd sort of way all this—with my son— has been good for me in that he has kept me from identifying totally with my job, giving all to work, as many doctors do. When I'm at work I'm constantly mindful that I have responsibilities elsewhere.'

'It gives you a balance,' she agreed. 'I get the sense, Guy, that you don't trust women very much. You want to, maybe, but can't really bring yourself to do it. Like most men—' she forced herself to go on '—you want a woman physically, but maybe not in any other way.'

He was silent for such long moments that Josey felt herself go hot with embarrassment, wondering whether she had made a big blunder. The need to know was uppermost. Once a man had kissed you, it changed things…

'You're right,' he said consideringly, at last. 'I do seem to have trouble trusting. What about you, Josey? You intrigue me. Tell me about yourself—if you want to, that is. Mac hinted at something.'

Josey let that pass. 'Oh, did she? I'm an emotional mess still,' she said with a self-deprecating laugh.

'I'll ask you the same question that you asked me—do you love him?'

'No,' she admitted, surprising herself a little. 'I was shattered because he destroyed my innocence, my confidence, my self-esteem, my willingness to give without expecting anything specific in return. Except his love.'

'How?' he said gently.

'I had to have an operation to remove some ovarian cysts. After that, when my ability to conceive was in question, he told me that he would never want to marry a woman who couldn't have a baby—even though marriage was something we had never talked about. He…he repudiated me when I was most vulnerable…' Her voice had lowered to a whisper, then haltingly she went on. 'Not that I really expected him to marry me, then or ever. Now I don't think I really wanted it either, it wouldn't have been right. It was the way he made me feel, that I was of no value, you see…'

'My God,' Guy said.

'I…I didn't think I would be able to tell you that. Just a few minutes ago I was thinking that I wouldn't easily be able to talk about it to a man, and now I've come out with it.' She laughed self-consciously. 'I don't usually blurt things out like that.'

'How do you know for sure that you couldn't have a baby?' he said.

'Well, I…don't know for sure, of course,' she said, her voice low and her cheeks burning. Hopefully he couldn't see that too clearly. In fact, after the operation she and Joe had never slept together again—and she hadn't had a sexual relationship with any other man since then. And she had always been protected against pregnancy when she had been with Joe.

Oddly, she felt that Guy could guess all that quite easily. After all, she didn't seem like the type of young woman who would go around trying to become pregnant to prove that she could. 'All this seems very particular to me, of course,' she said apologetically, 'but it's quite general, isn't it? If one looks at it in a statistical way.'

Guy eased himself round in his seat so that he was facing her, very close. Josey wanted to touch his face, to trace the outline of his mouth with her fingers. 'We can't do that, it's too personal,' he said softly. 'Forgive me if I sound facetious, Josey, I don't mean to be. If you want to know if you can become pregnant, it could be fun finding out.'

Guy took off his gloves and cupped her cheek warmly in his hand. 'You can call upon me any time,' he said huskily. To temper any suggestion that he might be making light of her problem, he touched her lips with little kisses, disarming her, somehow managing to convey to her that he was serious, that her situation was serious. In response, her heart began to beat with a deeper, faster rhythm.

'And what would happen then?' she ventured. If she were to take him up on that, and she became pregnant, what would he do?

'I would be prepared for the consequences,' he said, with a slow smile that totally disarmed her at that moment. No doubt common sense would prevail later, she thought as her face flamed with her own thoughts of wanting him. 'Of course, I've never sired a child. It doesn't matter so much, you know, Josey. A man could love you for yourself, without that.'

Their conversation was getting them into deep waters, and Josey didn't know what to say next. Instead, she swallowed the emotional lump in her throat, so intensely aware of him next to her, inches away, that she thought she might do something foolish, like throw herself at him, if she didn't go.

'But it wouldn't be fair somehow,' she said. 'It's so awkward, having to say something about it at the very beginning of really getting to know someone you like. Otherwise it would be false pretences somehow. Yet one can't presume early on that a particular man would want you anyway…permanently.'

They sat in silence for a while, both seemingly lost in thought. Josey held herself rigid, wanting to touch him.

'God, I'm tired,' he said, putting back his head, closing his eyes and stretching. 'You must be, too.'

'I must go,' she said hastily, making a move, feeling that he had changed the subject because he wanted to go.

'No!' His hand grasped her arm. 'Not yet, Josey. Will you agree to have dinner with me some time? Today didn't count.'

'Yes, I'd like to,' she said.

'I wanted you to know the complications of my life,' he said tiredly.

Words came to her lips that she hadn't planned. 'You could be using that as an excuse, Guy. An excuse not to get involved beyond a certain level.'

'Yes, I could. So could you, Josey.'

'Maybe. I don't mean to belittle your problems in any way, Guy,' she added hastily.

'Perhaps it's just that one gets more cynical, or maybe just more realistic. We grow up, in other words,' he said, more serious now.

'Mmm.'

'I have a sense of urgency, Josey. I want to get to know you before I have to leave Gresham General, before Alec Ramsay comes back. Unless he breaks another leg, there may not be much time.'

'I think I would like that,' she ventured quietly, smiling.

'Come here,' he said huskily, reaching for her, pulling her into his arms, as close as he could with their bulky coats in the way.

With Guy's left hand he turned off the engine of the car so that the headlights went off, together with the heater, while with his other hand he pushed off her hat so that he could twine his fingers in her hair and ease her head towards him, holding her captive, so that he could kiss her.

When his lips touched hers, Josey closed her eyes and gave herself up to the unexpected flare of desire that his touch aroused in her. Other men had kissed her since Joe, but it had been as though her emotions had been switched off, that she had been trapped in a pervading deadness. The sensation of Guy's fingers in her hair, softly caressing, contributed to the feeling of letting go. There was a tremendous sense of relief that she could still feel joy at a man's touch.

She slipped a hand out of her warm glove and touched his face, his rough cheek that was in need of a shave, then his damp hair. All thoughts of other men went from her mind as their mouths clung together. With eyes closed, everything else was blotted out but the feel of him, and she wanted that feeling to go on for a long, long time.

With the heater off in the car it didn't take long for the cold to penetrate the interior, and she shivered. Guy opened his huge coat and pulled her inside its folds, close to him, and wrapped it around her. 'Come here, come close to me. I don't want to let you go, Josey.'

'Oh, Guy…' She breathed the words against his face, then put her head on his shoulder.

'Josey, I didn't mean to do this,' he whispered as his lips moved over her neck, her face, his breathing uneven. 'I intended to go straight back. Do you mind?'

'No,' she whispered back, her eyes closed, delighting in being held by him, of feeling cherished, but at the same time she warned herself not to read too much into it.

A picture came to her then of what it might be like to sleep in Guy's arms. Instinctively she knew that she would want to be with him. He would have the ability to lose himself in her, and she in him… He wouldn't stand back mentally to watch himself performing. She was no longer a naïve girl. To have to wait until Monday to see him again seemed like for ever.

It was no good, she couldn't live in a fantasy world. He had to get back, should have left ten minutes ago. Rachel and Mrs Canning needed him back home. Urgently she put her arms up around his neck and pressed her mouth to his in a farewell kiss. 'I wish you could stay with me,' she breathed against his ear, 'but you have to go back to your children.'

'Yes, I know. I'll wait until you're inside the house.'

He picked up her hat, which had fallen to the floor, and put it on her head. 'Gloves?' he said.

'Here…' She scrabbled around at their feet to find her gloves. Taking them from her, he held them for her to put her hands in.

'I hope you'll dream of me,' he said. 'Go now, quickly, before I kidnap you.'

Awkwardly Josey scrambled out of the car into the raw cold, stepping down into snow that came up over her ankles. 'Goodnight, Guy,' she whispered. 'See you at work on Monday.'

'Yes.'

By the light of the headlamps she saw her way to her front door, waved him goodbye. Inside her warm, cosy flat she stripped off her outer things automatically, already missing him. To say that she felt mixed up was putting it mildly.

In her bedroom she looked at herself in the dressing-table mirror, at her pale face surrounded by dishevelled hair, her eyes wild. Then she sank down on the bed and began to laugh with an abandoned, slightly hysterical mirth. By having spent a rather strange evening with a very attractive and nice man, a very special man, having been kissed by him, then held for precious minutes in his arms, it felt as though she had done a lot to expunge Joe Falconer from her psyche. At least, for now. Maybe in the morning she would feel differently.

She lay down on the bed and put her hands behind her head. It was a relief to put her feet up. Now that the excitement was over she became more aware of her fatigue, her aching feet. Guy was like a prescription for a disease, a drug that had worked. Yet she had to be careful… In their own ways, neither one of them was free.

Joe had more or less told her that no young man would take on a woman who might have trouble becoming pregnant, even a man who wanted primarily a sexual relationship. At the time she had believed him. Now she wasn't sure about any of those things.

There was evidence that she was ovulating as her body had returned to at least a partial normal function after a few weeks from the operation. Those weeks of waiting had been horrendous, waiting for a period to indicate that she had ovulated earlier. During that time she had felt sick with worry, yet at the same time seeing the irony of the situation, when many woman were sick with worry because they *were* pregnant when they didn't want to be.

Josey turned on her side, clutching the pillow, thinking back, her mood of abandoned mirth changing to something more serious. She would never want to repeat those awful weeks after the operation, when she had thought of herself as less of a woman, as somehow of a neuter gender, all compounded by Joe's rejection of her, which she had mulled over obsessively. Still there was a nagging doubt, a terrible preoccupation with it, a loss of confidence.

Tears of tiredness and regret for things that had happened in the past formed in her eyes and spilled over onto the pillow. In moments of reality like this she knew that the relationship between herself and Joe hadn't been going anywhere even before she'd had the operation; she had known it then really in her heart of hearts, but hadn't wanted to face up to it.

The operation had brought her down to earth with a thump. Instinctively, goaded at last beyond endurance, she had known what to do to save herself, what had been best for her—to detach herself from Joe and his world as quickly as she could, a world in which she'd been a cog in the machinery that had made his life and his career work smoothly. He had certainly not counted the cost to her, had gradually taken her for granted. Alone she'd been forced to take account of what being with him had been costing her.

Now she had met Guy Lake, the first man to have broken her barrier of indifference. She was both exhilarated and frightened. Guy had asked her to dream of him. Yes, as far as that was controllable, she would bring him into her dreams.

Wiping the tears away, she found herself smiling again. It would be a long time before she could get him out of her mind.

# CHAPTER SIX

ON MONDAY morning, going to work in snow again, at a temperature of fifteen degrees below freezing, Josey had definitely come down to earth. Her boots crunched through snow that was no longer soft and fluffy, but frozen on the surface to a crisp, dry crust. On days like this she speculated about the cases that they were likely to get in the ER.

It had been a good weekend. On Saturday she had met up with Linda Sparks, and they had gone to an underground mall for lunch in central Gresham, again like moles getting away from the elements of nature. She had also spent a fair amount of time resting and catching up on sleep. Consequently her energy level was up.

Now, as she walked, she allowed herself to dwell on Guy again, having been shying away from thinking too much about him. She was looking forward to working with him again, although for the next few days she would be in medical emergency—with the heart attacks, influenza, pneumonia, unexplained abdominal pain, chest pain, uterine bleeding, diabetic comas.

The coffee-room was crowded as usual when she went into that pleasant, warm fug created by the smell of coffee and of muffins heated up in the microwave oven. She was wearing the usual crisp white lab coat over a blue scrub suit, and her comfortable white uniform shoes. Her hair, newly washed, was soft and shining.

'Hi, Linda,' she greeted her friend. 'Ready for the fray?'

'As ready as I'll ever be.' Linda was pale and blonde,

deceptively fragile-looking, but as tough as they came in that department. She seldom took any lip from anybody.

'Morning, Josey.' Todd joined her at the coffee-urn. 'Had a good weekend?'

'Wonderful. I slept a lot.'

'Ah, the urge to hibernate,' he said. 'A throwback to our primitive ancestors.'

'No, Todd, a throwback to normal.'

She knew exactly the moment that Guy came into the room—she could have sworn that the hairs on the back of her neck stood up. A wave of heat went through her as she recollected the way he had kissed her, held her with his coat wrapped around her. That experience had taken on the quality of myth.

She forced herself to look up casually as she moved away from the urn, seeking a quiet space to stand. His eyes met hers and he gave a quick smile of acknowledgement before moving away to get coffee. The last thing either of them wanted was for others to tune in to any vibes between them, but often the more one pretended casualness, the more obvious an emotional involvement became to others, so she wasn't going to pretend to ignore him.

Linda came to stand beside her. 'Well, I wonder how much of the hunky Dr Lake we'll see today,' Linda speculated.

'Not as much, I guess,' Josey replied. 'Pity. I was just getting used to him.'

'You can say that again.'

Linda left the room ahead of her, and as Josey washed her coffee-mug at the sink and put it away in the cupboard she knew that Guy would follow her as she left the room, so she took her time going out so that he could disengage himself.

'Josey!' he called softly after her when she was part way

down the corridor outside. 'I meant to ask for your phone number on Friday.' He came up to her swiftly and she could see that he looked more rested—his eyes were alight with the kind of interest that a full-blooded male showed when he liked a woman. 'Do you mind if I have your number?'

'No.' Taking a notebook and pen from her pocket, she quickly wrote the number down for him. 'How's Tom?'

'Subdued, but otherwise all right,' he said. 'I've asked the school to keep him there after classes until I or Mrs Canning can come to pick him up. They have a lot of after-school activities, fortunately. Rachel is in the same school, so she can travel with him.'

'I'm very glad,' she said sincerely, wondering how she herself would cope with such a responsibility and anxiety.

'May I call you some time in the evening?' he asked, pocketing the piece of paper.

Josey nodded, and stood to watch him walk away from her, just as Todd came along the corridor in the opposite direction having, no doubt, seen her hand Guy the piece of paper.

'Wow!' Todd said, stopping by her. 'He's a fast worker. Was that your phone number you gave him?' He made a face at her of mock surprise.

'It was, as a matter of fact.' She grinned at him. 'But don't spread it around, please. You know what a hotbed of gossip this place is.'

Todd laughed. 'I wouldn't be surprised if you're in a hot bed pretty soon. I thought he was interested in you last week.'

'You've got a prurient mind.' She laughed, spinning on her heel. 'See you later.'

The day started with a vengeance. Patients were lying on stretchers in the treatment rooms and in the corridors of the medical emergency section of the ER. Wading right into the fray, Josey took the top chart from a pile on the desk in the nurses' station, the pile indicating patients waiting to be seen, marked 'priority one'. On the top sheet the complaint, as described by the patient when he or she had come in, had been written by the triage nurse. Those patients who were deemed serious weren't left to wait long. All of them were placed in categories of urgency.

Her first patient was a fifty-eight-year-old construction worker, Dino Fernandez, who had centrally located chest pain extending to his left arm, and difficulty in breathing. He had just been brought in by his adult son.

'Good morning, Mr Fernandez,' Josey said. 'I'm a nurse and I'm going to take a quick look at you before the doctor comes.' Although the patient had a swarthy complexion, he had an underlying pallor and a whiteness around the mouth, typical of someone in pain and shock. 'Show me where the pain is and, please, tell me when it started.'

'Started this morning, five o'clock, when I got up to go to work,' he said. 'Suddenly. It's right here.' He touched the centre of his chest. 'It goes down my arm. It's very bad.' He grimaced to demonstrate the intensity of the pain.

'Does the pain come and go, or is it there all the time?'

'All the time,' he said. There was a sheen of sweat on his upper lip and on his forehead.

'We'll give you something for pain very soon,' she said, 'I just have to do a few things first.'

All the nurses and doctors in the ER knew that some people who were drug addicts were adept at mimicking heart-attack symptoms in order to get an injection of morphine or pethidine, so they all had to be careful. As Josey looked assessingly at Mr Fernandez, she didn't think he came into that category.

Quickly she made basic notes, then took his temperature, pulse rate and blood pressure and listened to his chest with her stethoscope for abnormal and irregular heart sounds. The patient was overweight. 'Do you smoke, Mr Fernandez?'

'Yes,' he said, his face tense with pain.

'How many and for how long?'

'Twenty a day, for…maybe twenty-five years,' he said, grunting a little, trying not to take a deep breath because expanding his chest was painful.

Josey pressed the intercom button for the triage station. 'Doctor to cubicle one, stat,' she said. Any doctor who was free would be there in moments. 'Priority one. And haematology tech or IV nurse, stat.' There were blood samples to be taken and sent to the lab.

'Am I having a heart attack?' Mr Fernandez asked.

'It's possible, Mr Fernandez,' Josey said carefully, doing everything calmly and deliberately, without undue haste. 'We have to do a few tests to find out, one way or the other. Have you had this sort of pain before?' She began to prepare the leads and electrodes of the electrocardiogram machine as she spoke.

'Well…yes, but not as bad as this, no way as bad,' Mr Fernandez admitted, panting. 'I always put it down to indigestion. That's all I need—a heart attack.'

'Just going to put these leads on your chest, and on your wrists and ankles,' Josey said soothingly. 'We'll take a graph of your heartbeat.'

She had it going when both the haematology tech and Guy arrived at the same time. 'Oh…Dr Lake,' she said, surprised to see him. 'Possible MI. He's in a lot of pain. Central chest pain radiating down the left arm. Pulse rate 122, respirations 28 per minute, blood pressure 159/95.

Smoking for twenty-five years. Pain started 5 a.m., constant, severe.'

'Hello, Mr Fernandez,' Guy greeted the patient, having glanced quickly at the chart and the graph. 'I'm Dr Lake, and this is the tech from the lab who's going to take some blood samples so that we can make a diagnosis. We'll give you something for the pain now.'

The man nodded, relieved.

While the haematology tech placed a rubber tourniquet around the man's arm in preparation to draw some blood from a vein, Guy looked more closely at the strip of graph paper that was coming out of the machine.

'I'll write an order for morphine and the anticoagulants,' he said to Josey quietly. 'Could you get those right away?' He looked at his wrist-watch. 'Already it's been two and a half hours since the pain started, according to the chart. If we don't give him that anti-clotting stuff right away it won't be effective—we probably won't wait for the lab result. In my experience, patients have usually had some pain considerably longer than they state.'

'Yes,' Josey agreed. 'I'll get the drugs.'

'I'll take a more detailed history. I'll put an IV line in while I'm talking to him.'

'Right,' she said, glad that it was him. 'I'll get the MI tray. Here's the IV equipment.'

Outside in the corridor, in a locked cupboard, were the myocardial infarction trays containing the drugs they would need for such a case. In seconds she was back with a tray, taking out the ampoules of morphine, together with a syringe and needle.

'I have to go to trauma room two when a patient comes in there—we're waiting for the ambulance to arrive,' Guy said, expertly inserting a butterfly cannula into a vein in the back of their patient's hand. 'But let me know when the creatine kinase results come back from the lab, would you?'

Now Guy was very professional, and Josey was glad of it. The experiences they had shared on Friday evening might never have taken place, except for a certain quiet understanding that, it seemed to Josey, was there between them.

'Yes,' she said. 'Shall I give intramuscular morphine?'

'Yes, I want to question him some more before he's out of it.'

'Is it a heart attack, Doctor?' Mr Fernandez asked again.

'We're not absolutely sure yet,' Guy said kindly. 'We have to get some test results back, but we're treating it as a mild heart attack, just to be on the safe side. We're going to give you a drug which will dissolve blood clots and prevent more forming, as a precaution.'

'This injection will take the pain away, Mr Fernandez,' Josey explained, 'and it will help you to relax.' While she gave the morphine, Guy injected the anticoagulants.

'Did you go to a doctor about your previous pain?' Guy asked, making his own notes.

'No. It went away, see,' the patient said. 'Please... where's my son? My son should be with me—he went to find a place to park his car. How will he know where to find me?'

'The nurse at the front desk will direct him, don't worry,' Josey said. 'I expect he'll be here in a few minutes.' While Guy was still taking the history, she took the opportunity to ready the oxygen mask and tubing.

'Did you take any sort of medication before you came into the hospital, Mr Fernandez?' Guy said, having listened to the man's chest.

'I took some antacid stuff—it didn't do any good,' he said. He closed his eyes, trying to hide his fear.

Guy came to stand by Josey. 'The ECG looks pretty conclusive,' he said quietly, showing her the last piece of graph paper from the electrocardiograph. They both knew that other medical conditions could mimic the symptoms of a heart attack, so they had to do some medical detective work to rule those out. 'I've given him the minimum dose of the anticoagulants until we get the blood results back.'

Josey nodded.

'Tell me, Mr Fernandez,' Guy said, 'did the pain become worse from 5 a.m., did it remain the same or become easier?'

'About the same,' Mr Fernandez answered. Josey noted that his speech was slightly slurred, his eyes becoming unfocussed, indications that the morphine was working.

Guy touched the man comfortingly on the arm for a moment. 'We're going to get someone to see you from the department of internal medicine, then we'll admit you to the hospital for a few days, probably to our coronary care unit. We'll explain to your son.'

Their patient relaxed back with a sigh and closed his eyes. 'Thank you,' he murmured.

He would most likely be in the hospital for more than a few days, Josey speculated, but they didn't want to add to his fear. A patient who was very frightened and in pain didn't take in all the information that was given to him, so one had to be careful to say only what was immediately necessary.

'Am I going to die?' He slurred the words.

'No, I very much doubt it,' Guy said. 'At the moment you're doing well, and everything's under control.'

Mr Fernandez nodded. 'My son…?' he whispered.

'We'll find him and get him to you,' Josey said. 'Don't worry.'

At that moment there was an announcement over the

paging system: 'Dr Guy Lake to trauma room two, please. Dr Guy Lake to trauma room two.'

Guy finished writing up his notes. 'I'll see you later, Mr Fernandez,' he said. 'The other doctor will be here in a moment. Josey, put a call through for the senior resident in internal medicine. And get Doug Randall in the meantime. Get him to draw up more of the anticoagulants in a syringe, have them ready for when we have the lab results. He can give them. And we'd better get a straight chest X-ray to see if there's any fluid in the lungs.' Quickly he signed a requisition form for the X-ray.

'OK,' she said. 'Thanks.'

At the door he turned back to her. 'And, Josey…take care. See you later,' he said very softly. As they looked at each other for those few seconds she saw the pupils of his eyes grow wider, and a very special smile of recognition lightened his features. A silent acknowledgement passed between them, then he was gone from her, striding down the corridor, his white lab coat flapping around his long legs. His need of her had flared unmistakably on his face, and she felt weak with the implications of it, the need to do something about it…

My God, what am I going to do about him? The words spoke themselves in Josey's mind, as though she had shouted them aloud, as she turned away. Then, with a supreme effort, she forced the image of Guy out of her mind and pressed the intercom button for the triage station. 'Dr Doug Randall and the senior internal medicine resident to cubicle one, please.'

'Gotcha,' a voice said at the other end.

Just then a man arrived at the cubicle entrance, escorted by an orderly. He was dressed in heavy outdoor clothing and looked very anxious, unmistakably Mr Fernandez's son. Josey smiled at him.

'Come in,' she said. 'He's all right.' She touched her patient's arm, bending down to him, noting that the lines of strain were easing from his face. 'Your son's here now, Mr Fernandez. Is the pain going away?'

He nodded.

The chest X-ray was done, the patient had been seen by the internal medicine resident, and Doug Randall made arrangements to admit him to the coronary care unit. 'That's the best place for him,' he explained to the son, 'because we have all the specialized equipment there and the special nurses. He'll be carefully monitored day and night.'

They were talking outside the cubicle, while Mr Fernandez slept under the influence of the morphine. 'Is he going to be all right?' The son asked. Josey's heart went out to him as he looked exhausted and extremely anxious.

'There's every indication that this is a mild attack,' Doug said reassuringly. 'A cardiologist will see him once he's in the unit, and we'll proceed from there. You can go up with him if you'd like to, see him settled.'

The son nodded. 'Yes, I'd like to. I'll have to call my mother, too.'

Two orderlies came to wheel Mr Fernandez to the CCU, and Josey gathered up all the paperwork. She would go with him up to the unit.

Late in the morning, almost time for lunch, Josey managed to get a belated coffee-break, and found that Linda was doing the same thing.

'So many people have this flu bug that's going around,' Linda said. 'I've just had a diabetic whose blood sugar is all out of kilter because she's been vomiting a lot. She's really dehydrated so she's been admitted.'

'Good. I hate seeing some of these patients sent home

when they should really be in hospital for several days at least,' Josey said.

'Yeah,' Linda agreed. 'When in doubt, admit.'

'Ah, caffeine!' Josey said ecstatically as she sipped her coffee.

'Are you planning to come to that party, Josey?' Linda asked. 'The Gresham teaching hospitals ER departments' two-yearly thing?'

'Toddy asked me that,' Josey said. 'I haven't decided yet. I'm not sure that I want to run into Joe.'

'Maybe that's just what you need,' Linda said. 'To see him and realize that he doesn't mean all that much to you any more. You maybe need to see the flesh-and-blood man, instead of living in a fantasy world of what might have been.'

'Maybe,' Josey said, sceptical. 'I'm just scared, Lindy.'

'Maybe Dr Lake will be there,' Linda said. 'I'll have to see if I can find an opportunity to ask him. Maybe a dance or two with him would help you to put Joe right out of your mind.'

'I don't suppose he would come alone,' Josey said. The fact that he had kissed her, several times, didn't preclude the probability that he had women available who would be only too happy to go with him to a party.

She felt a little odd not confiding in her friend about what had happened on the previous Friday evening, but she didn't want to gossip and since it had been a time of high emotion and anxiety, it wasn't typical of the usual interaction between a man and a woman who had recently met. Maybe she should just try to put it out of her mind and return to business as usual. Certainly she could have no claim to a special kind of intimacy with Guy, she told herself, even though there was very definitely a strong mutual attraction. Maybe that wouldn't last...

'You come to the party with me and Toddy and the rest of the gang,' Linda said, referring to the group within a group of the colleagues in the ER. 'We'll have a great time, and if necessary we'll form a protective ring around you if the great Joe Falconer appears.'

'That imagery is quite appealing.' Josey laughed. 'How could I resist?'

Back in medical emergency, there was a steady hum of human activity, staff moving quickly back and forth, patients moving in wheelchairs and on stretchers. Yet there was a sense that the pace had slowed a little from earlier in the morning, a certain frenetic edge had gone.

At the triage station Josey was about to take a folder off the pile when the nurse at the desk handed her one. 'Here's an interesting case for you, Josey,' she commented. 'Young guy, twenty-six, pyrexia of unknown origin. He's been waiting quite a while.'

'Oh, OK,' Josey said, accepting the file and flipping to the face sheet which contained the basic information about the patient. 'I haven't had a PUO for some time.'

Mentally she reviewed her knowledge of fever of unknown origin, as the condition was also called. Standing at the front desk, she read the gist of a long letter sent in by the patient's GP who had been treating him at home. PUO could be attributed to very many causes, the most common being infections and malignancy—cancer—with infections being the commoner. There were auto-immune diseases as well.

'What's your guess, Barb?' she said to the nurse.

'One has to think of AIDS,' the other nurse speculated, while she shuffled papers and typed on a computer, 'although the GP says in that letter he's HIV negative. Could be TB. Get Dr Lake to see him—here he is right now.'

'Hi, Barb. Hi, Josephine. How are you doing?' Guy came into the area and began to punch letters and numbers into a computer, looking for lab results, Josey decided. 'I have some free time now. Do you need me for something?'

'Well, I have this PUO case,' Josey said, feeling absurdly light-hearted because it was him. 'I know they can be complex, but I guess he'll have to be admitted, so maybe Doug Randall could deal with him.'

'How old is the patient?' he said.

'Twenty-six.' Josey gave him a quick outline of the case, her eyes going over Guy as she did so. He looked muscular and very fit in the green scrub suit, bare-headed, his dark hair flopping over his forehead as though he had run a hand through it many times. There was a quiet assurance in everything he did.

'I'll take a look at him,' he said. 'It will make a change for me. There seems to be a lull in the road traffic accidents.' After taking a printout from the computer, he came over to Josey to look at the letter she had been reading. 'I like to do a total body scan on these patients if there isn't anything immediately evident. Quite frequently with these cases there's a hidden source of infection,' he went on, 'even something like a tooth abscess, or a low-grade infection in bone from an old injury, or maybe something picked up from travel. It's usually better to admit them and do a whole battery of blood tests and other investigations.'

'Yes.' Josey had stiffened at his nearness, keeping her eyes on the letter, not wanting the astute Barb to pick up any vibes.

'Come on, Josephine,' he said, 'let's do a bit of detective work.'

'Don't you want me to do the preliminary work-up first?' she said.

'We'll do it together,' he said, taking her arm and beginning the walk to the patient's cubicle. 'It will be quicker that way. You can take blood while I ask all the questions.'

'Nobody calls me Josephine,' she said, looking up at him, trying to be very cool and not really succeeding. Barb, she knew, would be watching them, noting his hand on her arm.

'Good, because I like the name, very much. It will just be special to me, then.' He smiled down at her. 'Is that OK with you?'

Josey shrugged. 'Well, I guess,' she said, again faking nonchalance.

'Great,' he said. 'Now, let's see, this man's name is...Gary Clark.' They paused near the door of the treatment cubicle. 'The GP's letter says that he has a positive tuberculin skin test but not, he thinks, necessarily consistent with a current infection.'

'And the chest X-ray is clear,' Josey added.

'Hmm,' Guy murmured. 'He could have a TB kidney. Let's take a look at him.'

Gary Clark proved to be a thin, pale young man, whose facial bones jutted out prominently and whose large eyes were slightly sunken, as though he were dehydrated. Although he didn't look exactly sick, he didn't look entirely well either, Josey thought as she looked at him.

'Hello, Mr Clark, I'm Dr Lake,' Guy introduced himself, 'and this is Josey, the nurse who's going to take your temperature, blood pressure and so on. While she's doing that, I want to ask you some questions about your medical history and present condition.'

Gary Clark nodded tiredly.

Later, having taken a very detailed history, done a thorough examination of Mr Clark, including having taken blood for various tests, Guy decided to admit the man for observation and more tests.

'We'll get a scan done as soon as possible,' Guy said quietly to Josey as their patient was wheeled away to be admitted. 'I want to rule out tuberculosis and carcinoma. I've seen patients like him who have been diagnosed as neurotic, nothing wrong with them, then later it's become evident that they have small malignant tumours all over their body.'

'Let's hope not,' Josey said fervently.

At last the working day was over, and she was only twenty minutes late getting off duty. Before going home she wanted to pay quick visits to some of the patients who had passed through the ER over the past few days, to make sure they had survived. Selina Macintosh encouraged her nurses to do that, so they could see the results of the work they had done and learn from it.

In the specialized units she found first of all that the burns patients were still seriously ill, but expected to recover. The unknown man who had been beaten up was conscious now, but still unable or unwilling to give a name. Jason Laverne, who had had the ripped scalp, was still very bruised and swollen but otherwise doing well.

Lastly, she went to the CCU and saw that Dino Fernandez was comfortable. Of the four patients, he was the one who could recognize her, so she spoke to him for a few minutes. He seemed to have accepted that he had to remain in the hospital for a certain time, and he seemed relieved that he was receiving specialized treatment. As she walked away, she felt a certain contentment that they were all doing as well as one could have hoped for.

It was good to be off duty. These days what she really looked forward to doing was going home after work to her cosy flat, withdrawing to a certain extent, listening to music, reading, cooking herself good, simple food, drinking a glass of wine, waiting to heal.

Guy had said he would call her. Maybe he wanted to ask her to dinner, or maybe he just wanted to talk. Something different to look forward to.

# CHAPTER SEVEN

THE next two weeks went by very quickly, and on the Friday of the second week many of the nurses were looking forward to the multi-departmental party the following evening. It was to be held in the penthouse apartment of a surgeon from another hospital.

During all those two weeks Josey had been hoping that Guy would ask her to go with him to the party, but he hadn't done so. The disappointment that had built up from day to day had given way to a nagging frustration.

'It's in one of those super high-rise apartment buildings down near the waterfront,' Todd said to her after they had spent the day working together, 'and you're going to come, even if Linda and I have to frogmarch you there.'

'Oh, I'm going to come,' she said. 'I'm gearing myself up mentally for it. Thanks, Toddy, I really do appreciate it.'

'Great,' he said. 'I've got the taxi all lined up, so we'll be there at seven-thirty to pick you up. Right?'

'Right,' she said.

As she went off duty and then waited in the snow for the streetcar home, oddly glad of the cold wind that beat against her face and seemed to disperse the mental cobwebs that clouded her inner vision after a hard day, she found herself wondering again whether Guy would be there.

He still hadn't set a date for their dinner, and now she had the feeling that he was withdrawing from her, perhaps regretting, for reasons of his own, that he had shown a premature interest in her.

To be sure, he had called her the one time to explain to her a little more about his son, but he hadn't brought up anything very personal. She'd had the awful sinking feeling that she had blurted out too much about herself too soon. Now there was a sense of mourning where Guy was concerned, a feeling that something potentially lovely had been brought to a premature end. Yet at work she was aware that he looked at her, watched her a lot, so that sometimes she wanted to shout at him, Don't look at me if it doesn't mean anything.

On some days he had come to work looking drawn and haggard, and when she had asked after Tom, he had replied, 'Still giving a little cause for worry. Nothing that can't be handled.' During that time they hadn't spent another whole day working together, and when they had been together everything had been so rushed that there had been no time for any conversation other than remarks relating strictly to the job in hand.

The flu epidemic went on and on, not having yet reached a peak, it seemed. Quite a number of their flu patients had a secondary bacterial pneumonia which complicated the picture. All members of the staff were very, very tired. In contrast, it was great to have a party to look forward to, Josey thought as she got on the streetcar. Having decided to go, she was determined to enjoy herself. No one among her friends had been able to find out whether Guy intended to come…

'Wow! You look absolutely gorgeous!' Linda gasped as she stood, with Todd, on the doorstep of Josey's house on Saturday evening.

'Wow!' Todd echoed the sentiment.

In the background, on the street, the taxi waited for them, while snow whirled around in the lamplight. 'Come in before we all freeze,' Josey said, laughing. 'I just have to put my coat and boots on right here.'

Gratified by the response of her colleagues, Josey knew that she looked her best, having taken care with her appearance. There had been a new dress in her wardrobe which she had bought to attend some function with Joe but had never worn. Made of silk taffeta in a rich garnet red, it clung in artfully arranged diagonal folds to her figure and came down to just above her ankles, where it flared out slightly. In the artificial light the colour glowed. She had strappy sandals to match, and a shawl in the same fabric, with a long black silk fringe to give some warmth to her bare arms. Garnet earrings and a small black velvet evening shoulder bag completed the picture.

Linda and Todd came into her front hall while she put on boots and her heavy coat and put her other evening things in a bag. Her newly washed hair, with its red highlights, shiny and soft, was arranged in a profusion of large wispy curls that complemented the slightly nineteen-twenties look of her outfit.

'Ready!' she said. 'Let's go and have fun.'

'Yeah, right on!' Todd said. 'My motto has always been ''Work hard and play hard'' in this game.'

Linda and Todd each took an arm on either side of Josey and they walked out to the taxi. They both knew how her emotions were churning over the possibility of confronting Joe at the party. Yet, she thought, they didn't know how oddly churned up she was about the possibility of seeing Guy out of a work context. There was no way of knowing how she would react to him, and vice versa. Although she had known him for such a short while, she was disturbed by how much she cared…

The penthouse was on the twenty-third floor of a luxury apartment building, one of those places where the elevator went up silently and with great speed. As soon as they got out they heard the noise of music and loud conversation, and were enveloped in the crowd that had spilled out into a private small corridor. The guests were smart, sophisticated, Josey saw as she glanced around her. This was to be no beer-filled brawl, but something quite different.

She and Linda were shown to a bedroom where they could leave their coats, and as Josey exchanged her boots for the high-heeled sandals she caught sight of herself in a full-length mirror and was glad that she had dressed the way she had. Her eyes glowed, her hair shone and the dress complemented her slim yet curvaceous figure. Although not usually overly concerned about her appearance, she was pleased that she looked good, feeling her battered confidence rise a few notches. With an abandoned gesture, she flung the silk shawl around her shoulders.

Linda wore a short, strapless black dress in a charming lace, which complemented her blonde bob perfectly.

'You look adorable, Lindy,' Josey said sincerely. 'You'll get snapped up in no time.'

'I think we both look good,' Linda remarked, preening in front of the mirror. 'I don't believe in false modesty.'

'In that case,' Josey said, feeling almost sick with nerves, 'let's go and wow them.' After all, she hadn't set eyes on Joe for over eighteen months.

Some heads did turn as they entered the large main sitting room, which had an equally spacious dining room off it, accessible through an archway. Todd appeared, having waited for them. He wore a dinner jacket and bow-tie. Most of the other men present wore formal dress.

'I've discovered where the drinks are,' he said, 'and there are roving waiters, too. The food is out of this world.' He gestured towards the dining room. 'But let's get a drink first. There's another huge room where there's dancing.

This is going to be great fun. Take an arm, come on.' With a woman on each arm, he strutted to one end of the room where there were several bars set up, while the waiters carried trays of champagne.

'I'll have the punch first,' Josey said enthusiastically, catching sight of a generous-sized punch bowl filled with a pink liquid in which pieces of fruit and greenery floated. 'Then maybe I'll have champagne after.' Her mood was lifting. From another room they could hear music, something soft, slow and seductive.

Armed with glasses of punch, they moved towards the music, calling to friends and colleagues as they went.

'This is the life I was born for,' Todd said, sipping punch and nibbling on a canapé.

'Oh, yeah?' Lindy said. 'How come you're working in the ER, then?'

'Just biding my time. I'm going to dance with each of you in turn as soon as we've downed this punch,' Todd said.

Linda came to a halt. 'So he is here,' she breathed. 'I've just spotted Guy Lake.'

Josey didn't look round, she just finished her drink in a few determined gulps.

'You hang about here, Lindy, and maybe he'll spot you,' Todd said. 'I have to admit I'm madly jealous, all this drooling over him.'

'I don't like that word "drooling",' Linda said.

'Dance with me, then, Josey,' Todd said, putting down his drink. 'We'll leave Lindy to drool.'

They moved onto the polished wooden dance floor. There was a five-piece band, smooth, sophisticated.

'Does Lindy know you have something going with Dr Lake?' Todd asked when they were in the centre of the floor. 'She spends a lot of time trying to get his attention.'

'She doesn't know anything. But really, Toddy, I don't think I have anything going with him after all,' she said. 'He asked me out to dinner in a general way, and hasn't followed through yet.' She didn't want to tell him about Tom, it wasn't really her place to do so.

'Give the poor guy time,' he said.

'Well, I have the feeling the heat's off,' she said.

'You sound wistful.'

"I think maybe I am, but I'm not sure.'

The floor was filling up. At the far end of the room she could see that Linda had indeed cornered Guy, and a sharp stab of unfamiliar envy assailed her. She had been hugging to her the rather quaint idea that any intimacy he might have to share belonged to her.

She swallowed nervously as she looked at them and then away again quickly as Guy turned to face her and Todd. He looked devastatingly attractive, dressed in a dinner jacket, immaculate white shirt and black bow-tie. His slightly too long hair brushed his pristine collar at the back, and she had an urge to run her hands through that hair, to put her arms around his neck. Linda was looking up at him, talking animatedly.

When the music ended she stepped back from Todd. 'I'm going to get myself a glass of champagne,' she said, wanting to get out of the room for a few minutes to think about those proprietorial feelings, and those of envy. Most of the time she prided herself on never feeling envious of other people, especially friends. 'I'll be back.'

Shape up, girl, she told herself angrily as she smiled at Todd, knowing her smile was strained, then turned on her heel and walked back to the entrance to go to the bar, going as fast as her dress and her high heels would allow. The last thing she wanted was that Guy should think she had any particular feeling for him. A few kisses at a time of great stress didn't mean much, she thought…if anything. So he hadn't followed through with the dinner invitation. So what! His life was hectic, and it had been clear to her that he was having ongoing concerns with regard to his son. She had more or less told him that she wasn't available, and he had told her the same.

As she neared the entrance to the room she saw, to her horror, Joe Falconer coming in with a tall, thin, blonde woman with long, straight hair, one of those very sophisticated, anorexic-looking women who made the average normal woman feel like a hippopotamus. They were talking animatedly and Joe had a hand lightly, possessively, on her bare, almost skeletal arm.

Josey stopped, trying not to show on her face the alarm that she felt. Joe saw her a few seconds after she saw him. A look of surprise registered on his face as he recognized her, then a stunned look.

His glance, always so assessing, went over her from head to toe and back again three times, as though he was having difficulty taking in her appearance. This was more than the old Josey, she knew that with a small sense of triumph. Knowing him as well as she did, she could tell that he hadn't expected her to emerge as an attractive woman from the besotted girl who had been so in love with him.

'Hello, Joe,' she heard herself saying, sounding quite cool. 'How are you?' She actually put her hand out to him, like a member of a royal family, conferring honour, and watched him hesitate for a fraction of a second before he moved forward a pace to take it.

'Hello, Josey,' he said. 'Good to see you.' Yes, he definitely looked stunned, as though he hadn't taken into account the possibility that she might be there.

Liar! she wanted to say. Instead, she forced a smile to her lips. At close quarters she could see that he had aged, much more than she had thought he would have done. His face was tired and thin, his cheeks hollow, as though he had lost a lot of weight that he couldn't afford, and to her amazement she noted that his hair, the thick black curls, had thinned significantly, receding from the temples and forehead. Only the eyes and the tall, straight figure were the same—those eyes that could, with one look, make a woman's innards feel as though they were turning to jelly. Gratefully, she realized that they weren't having the old effect on her.

'This is Natasha,' he said, introducing the woman at his side. 'Natasha…Josey Lincoln. Natasha's my fiancée.'

'How do you do?' Josey said, feeling that rigid formality was in order as she clung to her dignity. From the polite, blank expression on the other woman's thin face as she murmured a vague greeting, Josey could tell that her name meant nothing. Joe hadn't told Natasha anything about her.

How quaint, Josey wanted to say. Well, I'm his former lover. We slept together, I cooked his meals, did his laundry, ran his household, while holding down a full time, demanding job, of course. And now I'm not even worth a mention.

'Excuse me,' she said, with another tight smile, feeling her jaw aching with the falsity of it, despising herself, even as she knew this wasn't the time or place to tell any home truths. It was all very much in the past now.

Blindly she turned back into the room, wanting to get away from them, and collided with someone. 'Josey,' a deep, caressing voice said, 'I've been waiting here patiently to have a dance with you.' Arms closed around her and she felt her face come up against a hard chest, a white shirt. Looking up, she saw Guy staring down at her, his face fixed with a bland smile.

'Hello, Falconer,' she heard him say above her, while

she determinedly kept her face averted. 'Still pulling in the women?'

Josey felt her jaw drop.

'This is my fiancée,' came the stiff reply. 'Natasha.'

'How do you do?' Guy murmured. 'You've got a great guy there.' The ambiguity in his tone was obvious, though subtle, so that Josey cringed, as well as wanting to laugh hysterically. Then Guy looked down at her. 'Will you do me the honour of this dance, Ms Lincoln?'

Blankly she went into his arms, suppressing the urge to laugh, which she could only attribute to the belated effects of the punch she had drunk. Moments ago she would have given a lot to be in those arms—now she felt mainly an immense sense of relief that she could get away from the 'cool' couple. How very cool and up to the minute they seemed. That was Joe all over. A saxophone dominated the sounds in the room, and Guy drew her close to him, not saying anything.

Deliberately she kept her head lowered so that she couldn't see Joe. Gradually a sobering coldness came over her, which she recognized as the beginning of the real end for herself and Joe. Actually seeing him with the other woman had done it. Oddly, he had looked taut and unrelaxed, which she didn't think had anything to do with her; he did not seem at all at ease with his fiancée. That unrelaxed quality made her remember how hard they had tried as a couple—because he had wanted it—to be in with a sophisticated, cool crowd, always doing the 'right' things socially. It had been such a relief, after the break-up, not to have to do that any more.

Nevertheless, a sadness signalled this process of ending. It was generally the same, this process, even though you knew that what you were doing was the right thing; there was a regret for the idealized version of what might have been, not for what actually had been. Suddenly she wanted that champagne very badly. At the same time it was so good to be in this man's arms.

'Are you very unhappy, Josey?' Guy broke the silence between them at last, speaking softly, bending down his head to her.

'No…not really. I'm relieved more than anything.' Josey looked up at him to meet eyes which were soft with an understanding that came from having personally experienced something similar, or so she fancied. 'I was like a child playing house, trying so hard to do everything, to make it work. I can see now that unless you are two equals, both pulling together, it isn't going to work.'

'Well, you're really off the hook now that he has a fiancée.' He bent down to her so that he could speak into her ear, against the sound of the music.

'Mmm,' she murmured.

'She's not as beautiful as you, Josey,' he murmured. There was an odd tension between them that Josey couldn't fathom, and she swallowed a sudden lump in her throat. If she could order an antidote to Joe Falconer it would be Guy Lake…and now here she was in his arms, gradually succumbing to his intense, understated, masculine presence. In spite of his words, she could sense a reserve in him, a holding back.

There were more people on the dance floor now, so that they had to move very close together. Guy put an arm warmly around her waist and held her against him so that they moved in perfect unison in time to the soft music.

She felt herself letting go, melting against him, so that everything other than the reality of him was gradually going from her mind, including Joe. Lights had been turned down. From the other rooms in the apartment there was a steady hum of conversation and laughter, a backdrop to the music.

Josey knew that tomorrow there would be gossip and spec-ulation about who had been with whom, and so on.

'Any other thoughts?' Guy murmured in her ear. 'Might as well get it off your chest while you're in a mind to do so. And I'm a captive audience.'

'A willing captive?'

'Mmm.'

'I wanted everything to be perfect,' she murmured back, her head close to his. If she were to turn her head just a little to the left, her lips would meet his…

'A common phenomenon,' he said dryly. 'Quite natural, too. That's nothing to castigate yourself for.'

'I tried to pretend that it *was* perfect, even when there was evidence to the contrary. Silly of me.'

'Sounds familiar. We all do that when we're young,' he said. 'You have the idea that if you can't save the world, you can at least ''save'' one person, i.e. make them happy. You fall in love. Emotions are so intense, but unfortu-nately—or fortunately in some cases—they don't always last long, not long enough for a permanent relationship to develop.'

'Is that what you did, Guy?' she said softly into his ear.

'I guess I did. Even when you know something isn't going to work, giving up on it is difficult,' he said.

'Yes,' she said, with heartfelt relief that he understood.

'Now I don't want to ''save'' anyone. I just try to honour the commitments that I have already.'

'I'm sure you do it well,' she said quietly. 'Now, what I very badly need is a glass of champagne, then I intend to enjoy the evening.' Although she meant every word, there was a somewhat fragile quality to her assertion.

Todd and Linda danced by and waved to Josey, with knowing looks on their faces, which made her wish they wouldn't be quite so transparent. Then she saw Mac, look-

ing amazingly attractive and feminine, dancing with one of
the more senior, highly respected surgeons.

'Come on,' Guy said, sliding a hand along her arm to
clasp her hand in his. 'Let's get out of this crush.'

In the next room they were offered champagne from a
silver tray, and Josey took a sip immediately. 'This is de-
licious,' she said appreciatively.

Guy had kept her hand, and now he drew her after him
as he walked away from the crush, out of the room, along
a narrow passage.

'Do you know this apartment, Guy?' she said.

'Yes. The owners are friends of mine.' He stated it flatly,
not trying to get any mileage out of the fact that the owners
were obviously fabulously rich. The apartment seemed to
take up the whole floor of the building.

He opened a door into a dark room, a bedroom—unused,
by the look of it. 'I want to get some fresh air,' he said.
'And short of going down twenty-three floors, this is the
only way.'

They crossed the room and Guy opened double french
doors and stepped onto a glassed-in balcony, like a con-
servatory, which was cool, some tiny windows being open
to the elements. Josey was aware, tensely, of a sense of
urgency in both of them.

Snow covered the top of the curved glass roof. The balcony was furnished for summer, with wicker chairs and a
sturdy chaise longue, and several little tables.

They stood at the window, looking north over the city at
the millions of twinkling lights spread out before them, a
vast panorama. At the other end of the balcony they could
look south over the dark expanse of the lake where they
couldn't see the other side.

'I guess this view compensates somewhat for not having
a garden, your own patch of land,' Josey said, talking too

quickly because she was nervous by his nearness now that they were alone. 'It's really spectacular, isn't it?' She drank the champagne eagerly, quickly, waiting for the gentle euphoria that it brought. Being totally alone with him made her realize how attracted she was to him, which made her sad because it seemed doomed from the outset.

'Yes.'

'I don't think I could live without a garden,' she said, still nervously aware that Guy was saying very little. 'I like to grow things, to muck about in the soil, to just go outside and be able to sit under a tree.'

The balcony room was cold, and she pulled her silk shawl close around her shoulders, shivering. Their breath made small clouds of vapour in the air. Guy took the glass out of her hand and put it on a table, then took off his jacket. 'Here,' he said, holding it for her to slip her arms into the sleeves, 'put this on. We won't stay long, it's pretty cool.'

'You'll freeze,' she said, liking the feel of the warm jacket, warm from his body, as she pulled it round her.

When Josey had the jacket on he took hold of the lapels and pulled her to him. 'Most of all, Josey,' he said huskily, 'I want to kiss you.'

When he enveloped her in his arms and his mouth came down hard on hers she thought she would faint with longing and the sensations he was arousing in her as she closed her eyes and swayed against him, surrendering herself to a pure physical pleasure that she hadn't felt for a long time. Because he was so tall and big she had to stand on tiptoe to put her arms around his neck, even though he bent down to her.

'Someone may come in here,' she whispered when they broke apart. 'Aren't we trespassing? Sort of?'

'I locked the balcony door when we came in,' he said.

'As for trespassing, I'm sure they wouldn't mind. It's a spare room. I've actually been a guest in it. Sometimes I keep an eye on the place when they go away, and they let me use it as a bolt hole.'

'Oh,' she said. 'And do you bring women here?'

'No,' he said, holding her against him.

'So I'm not one of many who have admired this view with you?' she persisted.

'No, Josey. Do you want to go back to the dance floor?'

More than anything she wanted to be with him like this, to be held by him, to feel like a normal woman again, with normal desires. In the last few months with Joe, when everything had been unravelling, she had felt unattractive, unloved, unwanted.

'No...' she said truthfully, turning to stare out of the window, letting him make of it what he would.

There was a tension of anticipation between them. In reply Guy took her hand, the intimate warmth of it making her suddenly extra vulnerable. She bit her lip, feeling an odd desire to cry. Holding someone's hand was such a simple gesture, yet one that seemed not common enough. It was a protective gesture and one of love and empathy, whether between parent and child, between lovers or a comforting gesture in times of extreme need, even from a stranger.

'What are you thinking?' he said.

'Wondering why we're here like this,' she said truthfully, not looking at him. 'It seems to mean something, but I know that it can't mean anything really. We're both too mixed up, in our own ways, not really free. We were talking just now of the young falling in love intensely. Well, I'm frightened of falling in love, Guy, of getting hurt again...'

'I can understand that,' he said. 'You mean with me?'

'Well…yes. You or anyone.' She added a qualifier, even though she only had him in mind.

There was a silence.

'It's true I'm not free, to live with anyone or to marry them—at least, not for a while,' he said at last, strain in his words. 'Josey, I want your company, very much. I hesitate because with you I know I'll want more. That may not be right for now, for either of us.'

'I didn't mean—' she began.

'I know,' he said, touching her face with his warm fingers.

'I like being with you,' she went on, 'talking to you, having you listen to me. It's such a pleasure. But I don't want to be confused by my own needs. What is it that you want, Guy?'

'I want your company, to talk,' he said huskily. Then he added, with a smile in his voice, 'And I want to lie with you in my arms in a warm place.'

Josey laughed. 'I see. I knew you were cold,' she said, her heart lifting, not wanting to consider too closely the implications of his words.

He chuckled, slipping a hand round her waist under the jacket. 'We're talking too much,' he said. This time she lifted up her face for him to kiss her, standing on tiptoe and putting her arms around his neck. With eyes closed, she let the feel of his mouth on hers pervade her whole being.

'Oh, God…Josey,' he murmured against her mouth, 'I also want to make love to you, for hours, to hold you.'

So it was out in the open now, what she had sensed. After all, it wasn't too difficult to know that he wanted her, she thought as she felt almost sick with her attraction to him, her longing for him. Common sense warned her to be careful. With Joe she had thought that she had been careful in the beginning, but she had been younger then, inexperienced.

He placed little sensual kisses on her lips, their mouths clinging, while she found her heart thudding with anticipation of something more. It felt as though every nerve end in her body was tingling with anticipation aroused by his touch.

Visions of lying with him in a large, warm bed filled her mind, and she put a hand behind his head to keep him to her. With a deep groan of pleasure he crushed her mouth with his, holding her strongly against him, the length of her body pressed against his. Through the fine cotton of his shirt she could feel his warm, firm flesh…

When they at last pulled apart, the sound of their breathing was loud in the silent room. With his arms around her, Guy moved his hands slowly, sensually over her body under his jacket, smoothing the thin silk of her dress.

'Any initiative must come from you, Josey.' He said the words against her cheek, holding his cheek against hers. 'I'm not going to force any issue. It wasn't my original intention to talk about warm beds—I don't want you to think that was why I brought you here.'

'You could have fooled me,' she said, grinning. 'You bring me to an icy room, take off your jacket so that I have to feel sorry for you, awaiting an offer for me to keep you warm.'

'Is that what I'm doing?' Guy smiled down at her.

'I suspect it is.'

In reply he wrapped her in his arms and gave her a bear hug.

'I'm serious,' he said, pulling away from her, to look out of the window again, an arm draped casually around her shoulders. 'It's over to you now. You can either see that as a burden or a freedom, or something just to dismiss.'

'Why me?'

'Right now I'm very burdened. I don't want to make that decision for someone else. In the end it's often an act of faith, but other considerations must come first. Like common sense,' he said.

'That's just what I was thinking,' Josey said.

Guy sighed, moving his hand up to stroke her neck gently. 'All I know at this moment is what I want,' he said. 'Trust is something that doesn't come easily to me any more.'

'That makes two of us, I guess,' she said softly. 'I regret it, but there it is.'

Josey looked down at the twinkling lights, her emotions and thoughts churning. Then she turned her head to kiss his hand, closing her eyes, trembling.

'Mmm, I like that,' he murmured, stroking her cheek with his thumb.

The emotional ball was very firmly in her court, it seemed. Yet he was giving her time; there was no real pressure. And he very definitely wanted her, an acknowledgement that made her feel as though her heart were singing. Even if they had no more than a physical relationship, she sensed that it would be wonderful. Also, she felt intuitively that Guy would be a friend to her, something Joe hadn't been. It was peculiar, really, that the truth hadn't come home to her until her time of dire need, that Joe had never been her friend.

'How's Tom?' she asked, forcing her mind away from her own needs.

'He's a lot better, getting back to normal, I think. Every time there's an episode with Tom—and there haven't been many yet, thank God,' he said, 'I'm reminded anew of what he means to me, how much he depends on me. I have no regrets whatsoever about being a father to him and to

Rachel, although there's a certain irony to that. I wanted to help the mother, I fell in love with her, in my idealistic way, and now I find myself father to two children who aren't actually my own. That's what it all means, really…being there for the other person, honouring the promises that you made, whether you verbalized them or not.'

'Mmm.'

'Easy to say, of course.'

'I can understand that,' Josey said. 'But does Tom expect you to…to sacrifice—if that's the right word—yourself for him? Maybe he doesn't see it in the same way. Maybe he could even feel guilty…'

'I hope he doesn't,' he said. 'He's my son and I love him—it's not a sacrifice for me. I want to do it. And a year or two from now, maybe I'll know what's what with him medically, psychologically.'

Josey wondered suddenly whether Guy was thinking, as she was, about the details of her private life that she, under the stress of the search for his son, had blurted out, as well as the details of her operation which had perhaps left her nearly infertile. Usually it took weeks or months for one to divulge such personal information. Now the weight of those intimate details seemed to hang between them, waiting, as it were, for other aspects of their relationship—if indeed there would be any relationship after tonight other than a professional one—to catch up.

'I think I shall be eternally grateful to you for helping me to see Joe for what he was…is,' she said, struggling for words. 'For helping me to take my mind off him. I don't think I shall ever see him again in the same way after hearing you say to him, "Still pulling in the women, Falconer?"' Josey laughed, looking up into Guy's face.

He laughed, too. 'Good,' he said emphatically, his arm still heavy on her shoulders. 'You know…I know quite a lot about your very personal life, on short acquaintance, but not much about other things, like your family, where you grew up—all that sort of stuff which helps us to understand the other person. I want to know everything about you.'

'I did feel a little embarrassed afterwards for saying those things…about the operation and so on,' she said, glad of the semi-darkness.

'You needn't have felt embarrassed,' he said. 'It's good to talk, one needs that.'

'I don't suppose you were the slightest bit interested in that,' she went on anyway, in an apologetic vein.

'We tend to exchange confidences in times of strain,' he said, looking out over the dark lake.

'Since then, I've felt that you're not always at ease with me,' she began again tentatively, 'so I thought perhaps I shouldn't have told you.'

'It was all right to tell me,' he said. 'If I seem not at ease, it's because I want what I suspect I can't have. Will you have dinner with me tomorrow night? I've put it off too long.'

Josey swallowed a nervous lump in her throat. With this man she was in danger of going from the proverbial frying-pan into the fire—she who had vowed a short while ago not to get involved with another man for a long time. In Guy Lake she thought she recognized something that she needed.

'Yes, I'd like that,' she said.

Abruptly she shrugged out of his jacket. There seemed nothing more to be said on that subject now, and she wanted to go before the rather delicate state of agreement that they seemed to have arrived at underwent any possible change. 'Maybe we should go back to the dance,' she said.

'Sure,' he said, putting on his jacket. 'Here, finish your drink first.' He handed her the half-finished glass of champagne and picked up his own as well. Clinking his glass against hers, he bent forward and kissed her on the mouth, the intimate touch arousing in her a longing to invite him back with her to her cosy flat, where they could light a fire against the cold, sit together...

As she sipped the liquid, which still had a few bubbles left in it, she suppressed the need as best she could. This wasn't the time for fantasy. If there were to be anything between herself and Guy, the time wasn't yet, she sensed, even though the image of Joe, with his dark, sexy eyes, was being replaced by the intense presence of this man, with his cool blue-grey eyes that were capable of showing tenderness, and his capacity for empathy and understanding. Could she dare to hope that they could mean something to each other, aside from the 'pleasant' company aspect and the sexual need?

'Let's go back,' Josey said softly.

On the crowded dance floor they became as anonymous as two people could be who also worked with some of those others. It seemed perfectly natural that they should stay together, there was no question of it. If there was to be nothing more for them after the dinner tomorrow, at least she could enjoy this.

# CHAPTER EIGHT

ON MONDAY Josey was working on the evening shift, which started at half past three and went to half past eleven, a time that could be very busy. She would be working that shift for the whole week, including the coming weekend, before getting two days off. Linda and Todd were also on the evening shift, working in surgical trauma, while she was in ambulatory care, dealing with the less life-threatening conditions but with a part of the service that was no less hectic.

'Hi, Josey,' Todd said to her as they all presented themselves just after three o'clock for the progress report from the departing day staff. 'I see you're with the walking wounded today.'

'Josey!' Linda addressed her with a muted shriek, then dropped her voice to a whisper. 'I've just been waiting to get the latest info about you and Guy. You monopolized him at that party, and I was green with envy!' She paused expectantly. 'I wanted to call you on the weekend, but I restrained myself.'

'Why should you have been green with envy when you had me?' Todd said.

'There's nothing to tell,' Josey whispered back.

'We noticed Joe,' Todd said, 'and his anorexic girlfriend. Completely flat-chested she was. Men tend to notice those things.'

'Women, too,' Linda said.

'Maybe that's why you broke up, Josey,' Todd said. 'He couldn't cope with your luscious curves.'

Josey grinned. 'Right on,' she said.

'Your first case is a dog bite,' Rex Chester, RN, the nurse at the triage station on the evening shift said to her after the report. 'He's in cubicle three…a middle-aged guy, got bitten a couple of places in the ass by one of those pit bull dogs. Just missed his scrotum.' He grinned wickedly. 'My guess is that he was being mean to the dog. That guy strikes me as a nasty piece of work, so be careful, Josey. Press the communication button if he gives you any trouble, and I'll come running.'

'You'd better come running, Chester,' she warned, flipping through the patient's chart, 'or I'll never speak to you again. This guy's been here before, I see.'

'He has—with the police in tow. Drunk and disorderly, got in a fight, and so on and so forth. What else is new?'

Chester was small, wiry, dark and intense, in contrast to Todd's pale tallness. Like Todd, he was great to work with, calm and competent.

'Which docs are on call?' Josey asked, scrutinizing the wall bulletin board behind Chester at the triage station desk on which the names of the evening shift doctors were written with black marker in large letters. 'Ah, the resident is Doug Randall, great! He's good to have on this shift.'

'Dr Lake's still here, doing a bit of sewing up in one of the trauma rooms,' Chester said, at which Josey's heart did a flip of recognition.

'Well, on with the fray, or whatever,' she said, leaving the triage station and striding down the corridor towards cubicle three in the ambulatory section of the ER.

Chester's mention of Guy triggered yet again her obsessive mulling over of the time she had spent with him the evening before, when they had gone out to dinner. They had talked a lot about many things, including her family— her parents, her one brother and two sisters—to whom she was very close. Sadly, they all lived far away from her now, in Vancouver.

Breezily she entered cubicle three through the open door, to stand beside the man who was reclining awkwardly on his side on the narrow examination bed there, his head propped up on one elbow. He was swarthy, greasy-haired, and far from clean in his person and clothing. Josey took all that in at one glance, feeling the certainty that came from experience that this man would be trouble. The small space was redolent of sweat and alcohol, with an overlay of vomit.

'Hello, Mr Harris,' she said, having noted that the man's name was Phil Harris. 'I'm the nurse. I'm going to take a look at you, clean up the wound a bit, then the doctor will come.'

'About bloody time,' the man said aggressively, drooling as he spoke. 'I've been waiting here about an hour. I'm in pain! Do you know that? Do you people even realize that?' He spat the words at her, releasing a spray of saliva so that Josey took a small step back. The man's eyelids drooped, both the upper and the lower, over his bloodshot eyes, so that he looked a little like a dog himself.

Josey consulted the admission sheet in the chart she was carrying to check the time he had arrived in the department. 'You came in twenty minutes ago, Mr Harris,' she said crisply, putting the chart down on the small trolley in the room and proceeding to open a general dressing tray which was already on the bedside table. The tray contained all that she would need for cleaning and exploring the wound superficially. 'We're sorry you had to wait that long, but we're getting on with it now. If you would pull down your pants and turn to face the wall, I can clean up the wounds. I understand you were bitten by a pit bull terrier.'

'Who told you that?' he said belligerently, suspiciously, as though it was all her fault. 'No, it was a Rottweiler.' Gingerly and grudgingly he turned so that he was on his other side, and eased down his pants. A filthy towel had been stuffed in his underpants, now soaked with blood.

Josey pulled on a pair of unsterile rubber gloves and put on her plastic goggles before she eased away the towel. 'Just going to remove the towel,' she said.

'Easy! Easy!' Phil Harris bawled.

Josey dropped the towel in a bin for hazardous waste. There were two bites, quite deep and extensive, in the man's buttocks. As she bent down to examine the wounds more closely she could count the teeth marks.

'You have two bites here, Mr Harris,' she said, striving to keep her voice neutral and professional, with just the right hint of authority. 'I'm going to do a superficial clean-up with a soap solution first, just to clean away the blood. For a deeper cleaning we'll have to irrigate the wounds where the teeth marks are, because they're quite deep. For that, I'll have to give you an injection of a painkiller, because it will be quite painful. The doctor will order something.'

'Injection? Injection?' he said, raising his voice and twisting his head round to look at her. 'You mean a needle?' There was an incredulous note in his voice.

'Yes,' Josey said crisply, discarding her used gloves and opening a pack of sterile gloves. With them on, she quickly sorted out her tray of instruments and dressings for the clean-up.

Phil Harris began to turn round slowly to face her. 'I can't stand needles,' he said. 'No way!'

'Well, that's the best way for us to make sure you don't have any pain while we're doing it,' Josey explained, knowing she would have to give him an intramuscular injection in the hip. There was no way that they would get an intravenous line in this man—he would raise blue murder, and the procedure didn't warrant that anyway.

'Please, turn towards the wall, Mr Harris,' she said patiently.

As the patient turned towards the wall he inadvertently plonked down on his injured buttocks. 'Aagh! Aagh!' he yelled. He let out a string of profanities while Josey helped him to turn over again, thus contaminating her sterile gloves.

'Try to relax,' she said soothingly as she changed her gloves. 'This won't hurt. As soon as I can clean up we'll put in a call for the doctor.'

Very carefully and gently she cleaned around the wounds, using an instrument and sterile gauze pads. Then she cleaned each puncture wound made by the teeth. These would have to be irrigated, probably with hydrogen peroxide, as they were more than superficial and could harbour bacteria that could later cause trouble.

'When we have someone with a dog bite we have to call the police, Mr Harris,' she explained, working away, 'so that they can contact the owner of the dog to make sure it has been vaccinated against rabies. Do you know who owns the dog?'

Again he twisted his head round to look at her, to fix her balefully with his bloodshot, watery eyes. Josey felt sorry for him. He must certainly have had an unpleasant experience, although, no doubt, the dog had received a kick or two. She thought of what Chester had said. Often a dog was provoked.

'It's my neighbour's dog,' he said. 'Rabies…' He considered, a different, incredulous note in his voice. 'You mean there's a chance I could have rabies?'

'It's not very likely,' Josey said soothingly, continuing her cleansing of the wounds. 'We just have to be on the safe side by checking with the owner.'

'You mean I could get rabies if that guy didn't get shots for his dog?' he persisted.

'You could if nothing was done about it,' Josey said, finishing the cleaning. In a moment she would put in a call for one of the doctors. 'But if we find that the dog hasn't been vaccinated, we can give you serum to prevent the disease.'

Phil Harris considered this carefully. 'That would mean more needles?' he queried at last, carefully turning back towards her.

'Yes, but it's unlikely—'

'I don't want more needles,' he shouted, glaring at her, 'I told you I can't stand 'em. I'll break every bone in his body if he didn't get that dog fixed.'

'Give me the neighbour's name and address, Mr Harris— and if you know the phone number, so much the better,' she said.

'"Give me the name and address, Mr Harris,"' he mimicked, his lips pursed up, making the utterance sound prissy in the extreme. 'No, I don't know the phone number. Why should I? I don't like him any more than I like his damn dog.'

Josey decided that it was time to call a halt to this behaviour, which would most likely only escalate. The sooner the police came to interview him, the better. They could stay while the staff completed the remainder of the treatment. The rabies issue was vital. There was no cure for rabies, once contracted.

Before Josey could press the page button for a doctor, Phil Harris had grabbed her by the forearm, his grip biting into her flesh. With his other hand he plucked up a pair of surgical scissors from the open tray. 'What do you think you're doing?' he shouted threateningly. With the scissors held like a knife, he made stabbing motions with them, close to her chest.

Keeping her cool, Josey looked at the man calmly, assessing the situation, and decided to say nothing to him. With the toe of her shoe she pressed a lever that was on the wall just above the floor, near the bed. The panic button was attached to an intercom in the triage area.

'Chester here!' a voice said immediately.

'Mayday,' she said calmly. 'Cubicle three.'

With a quick, supreme effort she jerked her arm upwards to break his grip, then stepped away from him. 'Put those scissors down, Mr Harris,' she said, 'otherwise you'll be charged with assault.'

He flung the scissors at her, then made a motion to get up.

'Lie down, Mr Harris,' she said loudly, with authority, and felt huge relief when he hesitated.

That hesitation gave her the precious moments she needed. She moved to the door and heard what sounded like the muted galloping of several horses. As Phil Harris heaved himself to a semi-sitting position and made to swing his legs off the table, bellowing with pain as he did so, the privacy curtain at the door was swished decisively aside and four men burst into the room. Josey saw Guy, Rex Chester, Doug Randall and a security man by the name of Jasper 'Tank' Mahoney.

A relieved grin of greeting spread across Josey's face as she saw this quartet. As she gazed on in admiration, she witnessed the men subdue Phil Harris in seconds with great expertise.

They swung him back onto the table then, as Mahoney leaned on the man's legs with his massive bulk, Guy got hold of him around the middle, Doug wrapped an arm around the man's neck, pinioning his head, and Chester got a strait-jacket onto his upper body before he knew what had happened. This was secured at the back, then in moments they had him immobile, flat on his back, with pressure on the dog bites. All the time he was yelling, 'Get away from me! Aagh! Aagh!'

While Guy and Chester took the body, standing right up against the table to brace themselves, Mahoney took both ankles in ham-like hands and Doug took the head. They nodded to one another, then with an expert, co-ordinated flip they turned the patient onto his side, facing the wall.

'Get your hands off me,' he bawled.

Not taking his hands off Phil Harris, Guy turned to look at Josey over his shoulder. 'Draw up 100 mg of pethidine, would you, Josey?' he said.

Josey nodded and went out, relieved that the episode was as good as over for now, although they had yet to finish the treatment and would have to keep the man for some time until he could be interviewed by police, which would have to wait until the effects of the drug had worn off. Pethidine was a very effective sedative and painkiller.

'We're going to give you something to take away the pain, Mr Harris,' Doug said when Josey came back in moments with the loaded syringe. 'Then we're going to get on with cleaning and dressing the wounds.'

While the other three put weight on the patient so that he couldn't move, effectively immobilized as he was in the upper part of his body, Guy injected the drug into the buttock, high up near the crest of the hip bone. It was relatively easy for him to do so as the skin was already exposed. Phil Harris started to swear again, and tried to bite Doug's hands, to which Doug responded by pushing his head down against the pillow so that he couldn't move it.

'Keep still and keep your mouth shut,' Guy demanded

sternly. 'Give the drug a chance to work. You'll feel better after.'

Josey relaxed, quietly going about the business of preparing for an irrigation of the wounds. 'This is a dog bite, Dr Lake,' she said, in case he hadn't had time to find out what the case had been all about before he had responded to the call for help. 'There are quite a lot of teeth marks, quite deep. Do you want me to do the irrigation?'

'Yes, you do it, Josey, you and Doug. We'll hold him until it's done, then we'll admit him, in restraints, overnight,' Guy said. 'We'd better write him up for some IM antibiotics. I don't suppose he'd take oral antibiotics once he's out of here, unless we put the fear of God into him.'

'He's already terrified of the rabies possibility,' Josey said, 'so maybe we can work on that.'

'Talking of rabies,' Chester said, 'I've already contacted the police with his name and address, but I couldn't get the name of the neighbour out of him about the dog. I guess the police will just go round to where he lives and find the neighbour and the vet who takes care of the dog—if there is one—and they should be back to us pretty soon.'

When Mr Harris gave a muffled snore, Guy released his grip. 'I have other things to finish up before I go home,' he said. 'Will you stay here, Doug? Mahoney? At least until this guy is tied down somewhere.'

Doug nodded. 'I'm free now,' he said. 'I'll write up the antibiotics.'

'I have to get back to the front,' Chester said, stepping back from the now inert patient. 'Are you OK, Josey? All in an evening's work, eh?'

'I'm all right,' she said. 'Thanks, guys, for responding so quickly. You sounded like a posse coming up the corridor.'

'I felt like a posse,' Chester said. 'Well, you take care,

and keep that jacket on the guy until the restraints are on in the bed.'

'I'll see to that,' Mahoney said stoically, his large presence reassuringly at the foot of the bed.

At the door, Guy gave Josey a slight smile. 'Maybe I'll talk to you before I go,' he said.

Not wanting the others to read anything into a verbal exchange between them, Josey nodded. 'Thank you, Dr Lake,' she said. All at once she wished she were going home with him, that she could get away, perhaps to have a long, leisurely dinner with him like the one they had shared the previous evening. Right now she was wondering whether she had imagined it all, a fantasy, so foreign did it seem to these surroundings.

The week ahead of the evening shift loomed long. When that was at an end she would definitely need those days off. Worst of all, she would see little of Guy, as he would be working during the day. He should have been off duty at four o'clock.

With the security man still holding the now snoring patient, Doug irrigated the wounds with hydrogen peroxide, with Josey's assistance, using a syringe with plastic tubing attached so that the fluid could get to the base of each puncture wound.

'That must be some dog,' Mahoney commented from his vantage point at the patient's ankles, where he kept two firm hands in place. 'My guess is that this guy was provoking the creature.'

'My thoughts entirely,' Josey said. 'He tried to stab me with a pair of scissors he snatched from the dressing tray.'

'Is that so?' Mahoney said. 'Well, later on I'll take a statement from you about what happened, and if he continues those tactics we'll get the police to charge him with something. These guys think they can get away with anything. Maybe it's the drink talking, but my guess is he's not exactly polite when he's stone cold sober.'

'If he ever is,' Doug said dryly.

They finished cleaning the wounds with an iodine solution.

'If you write up the order for the anti-tetanus shot, Dr Randall,' Josey said, 'I'll give it before he comes out of this.'

'Sure.'

Chester came back into the room. 'Hi,' he addressed them, 'I just got word from the police that the dog is OK, has had all its rabies shots. They checked with the vet.'

'That's great news, Chester,' Josey said. 'I wasn't looking forward to breaking it to him that he'd definitely need a series of very painful injections.'

'Not to mention giving them to him.' Chester grinned. 'How are you guys doing here?'

'Just about finished,' Doug said. 'Can you make the arrangements to transfer him for the night, Chester?'

'It's all done,' Chester said. 'I'll just get the porters to come down here with a stretcher. Well, I must get back to the front desk. See you guys later.'

It was a relief to get Mr Harris safely transported the short distance to the nearby overnight observation ward. No doubt he would discharge himself at the earliest opportunity, Josey speculated.

As she walked back towards the triage station a little later, passing as she did so a small waiting room in the ambulatory section, she saw a solitary figure, a teenage boy, sitting there. A few steps past the room Josey stopped. There had been something familiar about the boy, the way he had sat hunched forward, his head bent, with a mop of tousled dark hair that was thick on top and short at the sides. Surely that had been Tom, Guy's son?

After a second or two of indecision she carried on to the triage station. 'Anything else for me right now, Chester?' she asked, joining the him in the glass-walled office at one side of the large entrance lobby of the ER, from which vantage point all comings and goings could be seen, classified, documented and directed.

'Believe it or not, everything else is being taken care of right now. Take advantage of the lull and get yourself a cup of tea and a bite to eat,' Chester said. He sat at a curved desk in front of several computers and neat piles of forms and patient history sheets.

'I will,' she said. 'There's a boy sitting by himself in the waiting room along there.'

'Oh, that's Dr Lake's son. He's waiting for his dad.'

'You mean Dr Lake's still here?'

'Yep. We had this patient come in with bad chest pain, possible myocardial infarction. It's turned out to be cardiac tamponade. They're still working on him. I guess Dr Lake doesn't want to leave until the patient's ready to go up to the intensive care unit.'

Josey nodded. Cardiac tamponade was a very serious condition, in which there was an accumulation of fluid in the outer tissue layer of the heart, possibly caused by a viral infection such as influenza.

'Maybe I'll go and talk to Guy's son,' Josey said thoughtfully. 'I met him once. He must wonder what's taking so long.'

'Yeah, he could probably use a word. I didn't actually get a chance to tell Dr Lake he's here,' Chester said. 'I didn't want to butt in.'

Josey walked quickly back to the waiting room, half fearing that Tom would have disappeared. Chester wouldn't know, of course, about Tom's illness, or the family circumstances.

She smiled with relief, seeing him still there. He was sitting bent forward with his elbows on his knees, his chin propped up on his hands. 'Hello, Tom,' she said. 'I'm Josey Lincoln.'

'I remember you,' he said, straightening up. This time Josey got to look at him more thoroughly, seeing a thin, intelligent, sensitive face, at once sweetly boyish and mature beyond his years at the same time, very much like his sister.

'Your dad won't be long,' she said, hoping that was the case. 'He doesn't actually know you're here yet. I'm going to tell him. I was wondering if you would like to wait in his office. It's more comfortable there, and he has stuff there for making hot chocolate, coffee and so on.'

'OK,' he said, standing up. 'I am getting a bit fed up with waiting here. You're a nurse here?'

'Yes.'

In Guy's office she offered to make him hot chocolate. There was a single hotplate in the room, with a saucepan for heating milk.

'Great,' Tom said, brightening up as she quickly took milk from the small countertop refrigerator, opened the jar of cookies and efficiently began to prepare the hot drink, all the while keeping an eye on the time.

'Still lots of snow outside?' she said.

'Yeah, and it's still coming down,' he said. 'I had to keep an appointment downtown, so when it was over I just thought I'd wait for my dad. Mrs Canning came with me, then she left me here. We didn't think he would be this late.'

'No. Sometimes a case comes in that's very complex, and you can't just hand over to someone else until it gets to a certain point.'

'That's Dad all right,' Tom said, seating himself in a

comfortable chair. 'He likes to see things through.' There was a pride in his voice that made Josey's heart lift.

Mindful of the time, that she had a limited period in which to take a 'teabreak', she quickly made a mug of hot chocolate for Tom and a smaller cup for herself.

'Here, Tom,' she handed it to him. 'Help yourself to cookies, if you like.'

'Thanks. Of course, he's not my real dad,' Tom said, 'but I think of him as my real dad.'

'He told me,' Josey said, keeping her voice neutral. 'Have you met your real dad?'

'No…I've seen pictures of him. I expect I'll look for him one day, after I'm sixteen,' he said, 'just to satisfy myself that I don't care anything about him. My mother must know how to find him.'

'Yes. We need to confront the past sometimes,' she said, as much for herself as for him, admiring his courage. They sipped for a few moments in silence.

'Are you planning to go into medicine when you leave school?' she asked.

Tom shrugged. 'Who knows?' he said. 'I have no idea what I want to do. It bothers me sometimes.'

'It's normal at your age not to know, and it's probably better not to be too sure at this age anyway. Sometimes you can get locked into the wrong thing and then find that it's not so easy to get out, to change tracks. Keep your options open at your age—that's the most important—and focus on what really interests you, what you enjoy. Often a vocation comes out of what you enjoy, although it may not come immediately, not until you've had a wider experience of life, a variety of jobs.'

Suddenly Josey found that by talking to someone a lot younger than herself she could see things clearly by trying to help. If only someone had advised her before she had got so deeply involved with Joe. Would she have listened? Perhaps it would have depended on who had been giving the advice.

'Yeah. I don't think I would get into medicine. I'm not good enough at maths, physics, and chemistry. Don't want to, anyway. I like art, painting, drawing, photography.'

'Mmm,' Josey said, thinking how articulate he was, compared with the silent boy he had been the other time she had met him. He didn't seem depressed now...rather serious and thoughtful, perhaps. 'Go for what you like. Things will eventually fall into place.'

'The truth in one's mind comes out in the night,' he said solemnly, taking Josey by surprise, 'either in dreams or when you wake up really early. That in itself is a sign of clinical depression. I know that from what I've read. You wake up suddenly at three o'clock in the morning and you have tears in your eyes.'

Desperate to say the right thing, but not wanting to appear desperate, Josey looked at him and swallowed a lump of emotion that seemed to be blocking her throat.

'Has that ever happened to you?' he asked.

'Oh, yes,' she said, remembering, 'many times. More than I care to admit or think about. Perhaps those things are nature's way of helping us to sort things out when we're very mixed up. And we *do* sort them out. Only...when you're very young, a few weeks can seem like for ever.'

'Yeah,' he said feelingly.

'Do you like the school you're going to?' she asked.

'Yes, it's good, and the teachers I have for my courses are really great. There are some mediocrities, and some who know their stuff but can't teach. I've managed to avoid those.'

Josey smiled in commiseration and recognition of all the bad teachers, and the good, she had ever had, feeling a desire to giggle at his words. Tom smiled back. 'I know exactly what you mean,' she said.

'I have lots of friends there,' he said, 'and we have a good social life, like next Saturday we're having a party at someone's place because it's his birthday. I'm looking forward to that.'

'Well, Tom, I have to get back to work now, because I'm on the evening shift,' she said. 'I'll make sure your dad knows you're here. Don't leave without him.'

'I won't,' he said.

Josey had a longing to put her arms around the boy, to comfort him. I wish he were my son—the thought came to her as she looked at him from the doorway—and not just because Guy is his father.

As she walked away, the bitter realization came to her, as it had done many times, that she might never have a son, never have any children. Perhaps the most she could hope for would be to marry someone who already had children. Although she had never thought of herself as the earth-mother type, sometimes the longing to hold a baby in her arms, her own baby, came to her at unexpected moments, bringing with it pangs of regret so intense that she couldn't think of anything else.

Mindful that Tom could take off, even though he sounded very stable, she hurried along the corridor to the trauma rooms just in time to see a patient being wheeled out on a stretcher to go to the intensive care unit. Some of the day-shift nurses were still there. She stood for a few seconds viewing the chaos in the room left behind by the case as she searched the room for Guy. He was there, taking off his gloves and mask.

Josey went in, sidestepping buckets on wheels containing bloodstained gauze sponges and disposable plastic tubing, as well as equipment of all types.

'Dr Lake.' She went up to him. 'Tom's here, waiting for you in your office.'

His hair was rumpled from where he had raked off his operating cap, and his face was drawn and tired. Nonetheless, he looked alert. They had saved the patient's life in what could have been a missed diagnosis, she was aware of that.

'Hi, Josey.' He smiled, making her attraction to him come again very forcefully to the forefront of her mind. If only they weren't always so busy, if only they had more time to get to know one another... 'Long time no see, it seems,' he went on, his eyes going over her face as though he wanted to memorize each feature. 'And what is Tom doing in my office?'

Josey explained, smiling back at him involuntarily. 'I think he wants a ride home,' she ended up saying, wishing she were going with him.

Guy nodded. 'He had an appointment downtown. I guess Mrs, Canning thought he was all right to be left here. Well, I'm finished here, so we can go. I'm sorry I'm leaving you here, Josey.' He said the last words softly so that no one else could hear, the words sending a wave of heat over her.

'So am I,' she said truthfully.

'There will be other times,' he said, making it sound like a promise. 'How would you like to have a family dinner some time with us at my place? We can do the cooking, just the two of us. Give the kids a treat.'

'I'd love that.' She smiled, mindful that the other nurses were looking at her and Guy as they went about their business. 'That would be something to see, you cooking.'

'Yeah, I bet it would.' He gave her arm a quick squeeze. 'I hope you have a reasonable evening, Josey. Goodnight.' With another smile, he was gone, striding out of the room, calling as he went, 'Thank you, everyone. Goodnight.'

Getting away from curious stares, she left behind him. Feeling strangely bereft, and irritated with herself for feeling it, she hurried back towards the triage station. Not many days ago she had been telling herself that she should not get involved with Guy when he had expressed an interest in her. Now she wasn't at all sure that she had the option. The advent of his son's problems seemed to have put other interests largely on hold for him. She found that she was contrarily piqued.

'Hi,' Chester said to her when she presented herself at the triage station. 'I have another case for you—middle-aged woman with excessive uterine bleeding. I've put in a call for the gynae resident, she's on her way. Looks like a case for the operating rooms. She's already lost a lot of blood.'

'Right,' Josey said, taking the slim chart, her mind forging ahead to what she had to do for this woman. 'Makes a change from men with dog bites.'

'You said it!'

# CHAPTER NINE

THE remainder of the week until Saturday went by very quickly for Josey and the rest of the team in a blur of hectic work, sleeping late, getting up to do minimal housework and grocery shopping, before getting ready for work again. On the evening shift there wasn't much point in trying to lead a normal life. Social life had to be put on hold. On the plus side, there was no getting up at the crack of dawn to go to work in the biting cold.

Saturday evening was known as party night in the ER. For their patients, that was, not the staff. Both the evening shift and the better part of the night shift were usually busy, with a preponderance of road traffic accidents because of drivers under the influence of alcohol, and pedestrians coming from parties, wandering across streets and getting hit by cars. Then there were those who had been feeling ill all day, but had chosen to ignore it until late evening, who then became frightened at the prospect of a night ahead of not knowing what was wrong with them.

By ten-thirty on Saturday evening Josey felt very tired, knowing she was managing to keep going on surges of adrenaline—so she told herself grimly as she strode to the triage station to see how many cases were remaining. There was time for her to deal with one more case before she went off duty, or two or three lesser cases. Her feet were killing her, her legs ached and she longed to ease off her shoes, to go outside to feel the cold night air on her face. After a while the intense pace of the job got to you.

Linda Sparks was the triage nurse of the moment, while

Rex Chester was working the floor. 'Hi, Lindy.' Josey smiled tiredly at her friend. 'Anything else on the agenda for us? Or can I revert to going-home mode?'

'Don't relax just yet, kid,' Linda said, shuffling papers. 'The guys in the trauma rooms are expecting an accident case—four teenagers in a mild car accident, if one can call those mild—while you've got two ambulance cases coming in…someone who collapsed on the street, probable CVA, and a teenager with acute alcohol poisoning.'

'Someone partying who drank too much?' Josey asked. The other case, cardiovascular accident, CVA for short, meant a stroke.

'That's part of it, by the sound of things. But there seems to be more to it than that, according to the paramedics. He's on some sort of medication, too, and probably shouldn't have been drinking alcohol at all,' Linda said.

'Shall I take that case?'

'Yes, it looks like that will be the first one to get here,' Linda confirmed. 'You and Doug Randall can deal with it. The patient's unconscious, but breathing OK.'

Josey hurried off to prepare a treatment room. Quickly she set up two IV lines, with the bags of fluid, then opened a tray with the equipment for a stomach washout.

Doug came in just as she was ready. 'Hi, Josey,' he said. 'Looks like we won't get off on time tonight, eh?' He wore a crumpled green scrub suit and, like her, looked tired. 'I'd like an intubation tray on hand in case he gets into breathing difficulties. Sounds like he's out of it, but breathing OK right now. These young people frequently choke on their vomit, as I'm sure you know.'

'Yes. I've got the intubation tray,' she said, rushing about to get ready. 'Shall I put in the IV while you deal with the gastric lavage?'

'Sounds good to me,' Doug said.

Just as they were ready, the patient was brought in on a stretcher by two paramedics, wheeling past the triage station with a quick acknowledging wave and a gesture from Linda towards the treatment room where Josey stood waiting in the doorway. There was no time for a more formal checking-in.

The boy on the stretcher, coming in head first, was dark haired and pale. There was a plastic naso-pharangeal airway in his mouth to keep the airway open. The paramedics lifted the boy onto the treatment room table, while Josey and Doug stood back out of the way.

Then, as Josey moved forward, a horrible realization flooded over her. She recognized the face, the tousled, short, dark hair. 'Oh, God,' she said. 'Oh my God!'

'What is it?' Doug said sharply, coming to stand beside her as the paramedics deftly moved their stretcher out of the way and removed the bulky blankets and insulating cover.

'It's Tom,' she said, feeling sick, 'Tom Lake...Dr Lake's son.'

'That's right,' one of the paramedics said. 'His name's Tom Lake. Do you know him?'

'Oh, my God,' she said again, feeling a rare moment of panic. 'Yes...I know him...not very well. Is he all right? And does anyone know in his family?' Her thoughts went frantically to Guy. 'He's under age, only fifteen.'

'Not as far as we know. The police will do it, as this was an emergency call. A friend came in the ambulance with him. They were more intent on getting him here than informing the family.'

'We'll do it. His father works here,' Doug said tersely, moving in to take over. 'Come on, Josey, let's get to work on him. When you've got the IV in, go to phone Guy. It's better if it comes from one of us.'

Josey nodded, moving in quickly to record Tom's vital signs—blood pressure, pulse rate, respiration rate—while Doug began right away to insert a mouth gag and get the stomach tube down. All the time she felt sick with shock and anxiety, wanting to weep.

'His pressure's OK,' she said. 'A bit low, but OK.' She connected the automatic cardiac monitor and the blood-pressure cuff which would record those signs constantly and display them on a computer screen. While she wanted to rush out to telephone Guy, she forced herself to go through the prescribed routine for such a case in a calm, efficient manner. The first priority was to bring Tom to consciousness, to eliminate the alcohol from his body as quickly as possible.

Swallowing her anxiety, she tied a rubber tourniquet around Tom's arm to stem the flow of blood and bring up a vein in the back of his hand. As she bent her head to the task, slipping a butterfly needle and cannula into a vein, she prayed that everything would be all right. She connected the IV tubing from the bag of fluid to the cannula, and turned on the flow.

'I'll keep an eye on that,' Doug said, not pausing in the stomach lavage procedure. 'Call Guy.'

Josey hurried out of the room to an external telephone which was just outside in a corridor. All the telephone numbers of the departmental doctors, plus those of the consultants they used frequently, were displayed prominently on a sheet by the phone. Aware that her hands were shaking slightly, she took a deep breath and punched in Guy's number. Maybe by now he would be in bed.

'Hello, Dr Lake here,' he answered after only two rings, sounding as though he had been sleeping.

'Guy, it's Josey calling from the ER. I'm calling to say that we have Tom here.' Not waiting for him to say anything more, she quickly went over what they knew so far. 'He's all right, his vitals are stable,' she added. 'We're in the middle of the lavage now.'

'Hell!' Guy said, expelling a pent-up breath on a long sigh. 'I'll be right over. I understood he was staying the night at the friend's place, so I wasn't concerned that he wasn't home.' He paused. 'Damn, damn, damn! I should have checked up on him. He shouldn't be drinking and certainly not while he's on that medication. He's not out of it yet, though?'

'No. Maybe it was unintentional,' she said, expressing what she had been thinking. 'Maybe someone gave it to him, mixed with something else. Tom seems far too sensible to drink.' They both knew that he might have taken it deliberately because he was depressed, but her gut feeling told her otherwise.

He sighed again. 'Let's hope so,' he said heavily. 'Thank you for calling me, Josey. I appreciate hearing it from you. I'll see you in a short while.'

'Yes.'

When she got back to the room Doug looked up. 'He's responding,' he said to her. 'He's gagging a bit.'

The relief was intense, so that Josey felt like bursting into tears. They both stood at the end of the treatment table behind their patient's head, while Doug supported the stomach tube that was protruding from Tom's mouth. 'The washings are coming back quite clear now,' Doug said, 'so I'm going to remove the tube. He had no food in his stomach at all. Maybe that was good from the point of view of vomiting, and that may partially account for the fact that he succumbed to the alcohol so quickly.'

'Dr Lake's coming in,' Josey said, as she checked the rate of flow on the IV line, then checked the vital signs on the monitor. They were giving him dextrose and saline, a sugar and salt solution.

Carefully Doug clamped the stomach tube with artery forceps, then withdrew it from the stomach. As he did so, Tom gave a small muffled cough and his eyelids fluttered but didn't open. Now his stomach was empty.

'Tom! Tom! Open your eyes,' Josey said, raising her voice. Tom made a sound, while again his eyelids fluttered but didn't open completely. 'I'm so relieved I could weep,' she added to Doug.

'He'll be all right now,' Doug said, obvious relief in his voice. 'You know, I had no idea that Guy had a teenage son.'

It was now after the time Josey had been due to go off duty. When Guy came in, dressed in heavy outdoor clothing, with snow on his bare head and on his shoulders, she was sitting beside Tom. They had turned him on his side in the recovery position to maintain his airway and ensure that any secretions from his stomach and lungs would flow out of his mouth. He was still hooked up to the monitors.

For the past little while she had been holding his hand and talking to him. 'Tom, open your eyes, squeeze my fingers.' Sluggishly he had responded. Now, with Guy beside her, she wanted to stand up and fling her arms around his neck.

Forcing herself to remain seated, she looked up at him. 'He's conscious now,' she said. 'Responding quite a bit.'

'Thank God,' he said. Bending down to Tom so that his face was a few inches away from that of his son, he raised his voice. 'Tom…it's Dad. Open your eyes.'

Obediently Tom opened his eyes, his gaze poorly focussed. 'Josey?' The voice was slurred, barely audible.

'He must be all right…' Josey smiled up at Guy '…if he can recognize someone he doesn't know very well.'

A slight smile lightened Guy's haggard face, and his eyes scanned the monitors and the IV line. 'Saved one more time,' he said quietly. 'He's like a cat with nine lives.'

'Yes, it's me, Tom,' Josey said. 'You're in the emergency department. You're all right.'

'Josey? Dad?'

'Yes, it's me, son,' Guy said. He put his hand on Josey's shoulder. 'Will you stay a while longer, please? I'd appreciate having you here—and I can tell that Tom would. I'll drive you home, if you can stay.'

'I'd like to stay, Guy,' she said. 'There's no way I could go home now.'

Unexpectedly he bent down and kissed her on the cheek, then kissed Tom also. The sight of this large man bending down to kiss his son, in humility and gratitude, made tears prick her eyes and she bit her lip, looking down. His cheek had been cold against hers, cold from snow and wind and perhaps from that sick, paralysing fear that all normal people experienced when someone they loved was in danger.

'I had second thoughts about letting him go to this party, but you know how it is. It was given by a good friend of his…all his other close friends were going,' Guy said, looking down at his son with regret in his voice. 'He's been so much better recently. He seemed to be coming out of this particular bout of depression. He was so looking forward to this.'

'Yes, I know he was,' Josey said. 'He told me about it.'

'I'd better go and speak to Doug,' Guy said. 'I'll be back in a few minutes.'

When he had gone Josey let the tears seep from under her lids and wet her cheeks. Quietly she sat down again beside Tom. Now that she was officially off duty, he was the responsibility of the night nurses, but they had been grateful that she had agreed to stay until Guy arrived.

Taking a paper tissue from her pocket, she dabbed at her eyes.

Bone-weary, she knew that her tears were in part the tears of exhaustion, but they were also for the boy and for the man with whom she was involved emotionally. There was no denying it now.

How could a mother walk away and leave her children? Perhaps she had been able to go because she had known they would be well taken care of. Or maybe—a less palatable consideration—she hadn't cared enough.

It wasn't surprising really that Guy couldn't wholeheartedly trust a woman. Here she was herself, a woman who perhaps couldn't have children, sitting with a boy whose mother hadn't wanted him enough to stay with him. That was one of the many ironies and contradictions of life. Maybe she was just simplifying it all too much…

Later, in the middle of the night, Josey and Guy left the hospital together, walking to the parking lot. Their boots crunched on frozen snow and there was a bitter wind. Josey hardly noticed. Tom was fully conscious now and had spoken to Guy, while she had retreated into the background and the night nurses in the acute care unit had taken over.

'He said it was an accident,' Guy said, 'and I believe him. He drank what he thought was fruit punch and only found out a bit later, when he began to feel strange, that there had been vodka in it. How those kids get hold of the stuff, I don't know. I guess the parents were out when it happened.'

'It's a relief,' she said.

Driving through the snow-filled, silent streets was a cathartic experience for both of them, occupied as they were by their own thoughts. It seemed to her that Guy would always feel responsible for Tom, even though Tom was clearly an intelligent young man. His illness could be at least a partial handicap until medical research could come up with better drugs to help him. It seemed to her that Guy hadn't yet accepted that, as far as she could tell…accepted it enough to let other people into his life in more than a superficial way. Not that she could talk, of course, she told herself ruefully. If anyone was uptight, it was she, obsessively mulling over the past.

When Guy stopped the car at her home, turned off the engine, she knew that he would take her into his arms. Silently she turned to him and raised her face to his, closing her eyes in surrender and with longing when his mouth came down on hers. There was a desperation in him to which she responded with needs of her own. Joe Falconer had never meant as little to her as he did now. In moments her hands were in his hair, caressing him, as she kissed him back so that he could have no doubt of her feelings.

He had to get back to the hospital, having promised Tom he would be back. As he had said, he would never sleep now, so he wanted to sit with Tom until the morning. This was a stolen interlude away from duty of a different sort, the duty of paternal love, and they clung together. For now, she had to make do with fantasy. As surely as they were in each other's arms, she knew that she didn't want it to remain a fantasy.

'Josey…' he whispered her name, breaking away. 'I'll walk you to your door. I don't want to leave you. You know…when you're seeing dramatic things, day in and day out, having to deal with them, it's easy to give less importance to the other everyday aspects of normal life outside a hospital. It becomes a habit—the loss of family life, love, the ordinary things that people do, having fun, finding enjoyment in simple things. Crazy, really.'

Feeling oddly vulnerable, wanting to cry, she fussily

gathered together her work bag and her gloves, fumbling for the doorkey in her coat pocket, not trusting her voice.

At the door he waited while she unlocked it. 'When is your next day off?' he asked.

'I'm off Monday and Tuesday,' she said, not wanting him to go.

'I expect you spend the better part of Monday sleeping?' he said.

'Usually,' she agreed. 'I try to go out in the evening, making up for lost time.' She laughed, trying to hide her longing, not wanting to ask him outright why he wanted to know her days off.

Again he kissed her, lingeringly, on the mouth. 'You'd better go in before you freeze,' he said huskily. 'May I call you tomorrow, just before you leave to go to the hospital?'

'Yes, please, do,' she said. 'I...I'll want to know how Tom's doing before I get there.' Her voice trembled, and somehow she was having difficulty getting the words out. What, she wondered, do these kisses mean, if anything? Most men who liked women would take an opportunity to kiss an attractive woman, especially one who kissed back, wasn't passive.

'Goodnight,' he said, stepping back from her. 'Thank you for what you've done, over and above the line of duty.'

Then he was going away from her, crunching over the snow on her garden path. 'Guy!' she called after him. Stay with me, she wanted to say, spend the night with me, what's left of it...

He stood looking back at her. Of course, she didn't say that. 'Guy...don't...don't be a stranger,' she said.

For a moment she thought he would come back to her, sweep her up into his arms like Rhett Butler in *Gone With the Wind* and carry her up the short staircase to her bedroom. Instead, he gave her a slow smile. Yet the hesitation was palpable, as was their mutual sexual attraction. The reality of Tom as a patient stood between them, with Guy's need and obligation to get back to the hospital. The time ahead would be frightening for Tom, when the full realization came to him that he could have died. Josey knew that Guy would want to be there so that he was the person Tom saw every time he opened his eyes during that night.

Then he answered her entreaty. 'I won't be,' he said softly.

# CHAPTER TEN

THE telephone rang at 11 a.m. the next morning in Josey's flat, just as she was getting up. Sensing that it was Guy, she answered it quickly.

'Hello,' he said. 'I hope I didn't wake you, Josey. I held off as long as I could.'

'Hello, Guy,' she said, her heart lifting at the sound of his voice. 'No, you didn't wake me, I was up. I was hoping you would call, because I want to know how Tom is doing.' There was anxiety in her, like a sickness, in case the boy had experienced complications to do with the medications he was taking, but somehow she could tell from Guy's voice that nothing untoward had happened during the night.

It was strange how quickly she had come to feel that the welfare of this family had a lot to do with her, as though she were a part of it. There was a poignant longing to be with her own family, so close emotionally yet so far away physically. Perhaps they had been separated too long. It was time for a visit, a renewal.

'He's all right,' Guy said, his voice tired but replete with a profound relief. 'It's amazing how he's bounced back. According to him, the amount of alcohol he drank must have been very small, but combined with his medication it was enough to render him unconscious.'

'I'm so glad. I guess he won't be doing that again in a hurry.' Josey grinned, responding to the optimism she could hear in Guy's voice.

'No. I feel I can breathe easy again,' Guy said. 'Tom was lucid enough for us to have a long talk, and he's pretty mad with the boys who put vodka in a fruit punch without telling anybody. The parents of the boy who had the party have been on to me—they feel pretty awful.'

'I bet they do,' she said feelingly.

'I'm calling to see how you are—you must be tired,' he said. 'I stayed with Tom in his room, managed to lie down on the other bed and get some sleep.'

'I'm all right,' she said.

'Could you possibly come in to work half an hour early, Josey? I know it's a lot to ask, but Tom has asked especially to see you,' he said.

'I can do that,' she said. 'I…I'm pleased he wants to see me.'

'I could come to get you, if that would make it easier.'

'Thanks.'

Tom was in a two-bedded side room, the second bed empty, in the acute care unit. Josey stood with Guy beside the bed. Apart from an obvious tiredness, Tom was awake and apparently mentally alert. Intravenous fluids were still dripping into the vein in the back of his hand.

'How are you?' she said, touching his hand in commiseration, her eyes going over the IV line in the inevitable professional way that one had. 'I bet you've got the grandaddy of all headaches, Tom.'

'You're right there,' Tom agreed, giving a good imitation of a sheepish grin. 'I never knew what a hangover was before, and I sure hope never to experience it again. This fluid's helping a lot. Dr Randall said it's a matter of flushing the alcohol out of my body and I'll feel pretty good after that. It's much better than it was, there can't be much left in me. Anyway, sit down, Dad, Josey.' They sat, as requested, side by side, near the bed.

Having satisfied herself that he was all right, Josey had

to keep an eye on the time. 'I have to go to work again soon, Tom. I'll look in later, if I can,' she said.

Tom pulled himself to a better sitting position and looked at them, clearing his throat as he did so. His eyes had a slightly glazed look, and his speech was very slightly slurred, yet his mental faculties seemed clear. 'There's something I want to say to both of you,' he said, his pale face flushing a little. 'Now this has happened to me, I don't want to put off saying it.'

Guy was very still. 'Go on,' he said.

'Why don't you two get together?' Tom said. 'I know you want to…at least, I know you want to, Dad. Rachel knows it, too, and we've talked about it. We've seen the way you look at each other, and we're not stupid. Your body language gives you away as well. And Mrs Canning knows something's up.'

Out of the mouths of babes—or near-babes, Josey thought. And they had thought they were being so careful, so sophisticated, in keeping their attraction from others, especially Tom and Rachel. Perhaps they had been merely patronizing. She felt the familiar blush coming into her cheeks, and she couldn't look at Guy. They had both been put on the spot by this utterance.

'Um…I guess you're right, Tom,' Guy said.

'Don't ever use me as an excuse not to do something, Dad. And, Josey, don't let him use me as an excuse,' Tom said earnestly, looking from one to the other, his face taut with the determination to say what he had to say. 'I don't want that on my conscience…I couldn't bear it. Not on top of the other things I have to deal with.'

'I'll try not to,' Guy said, obviously moved and taken aback.

Josey decided to keep her mouth shut.

Tom carried on, rushing into further speech. 'I don't

want to talk in jargon, I want to put it the way I feel it. What I mean is, I don't want to be used like an object, so that you can say that I'm stopping you doing things. If you do that, I'll leave home when I'm in a fully rational mood, and even you won't be able to find me, Dad. I have friends.'

Guy's face was strained when Josey shot a sideways look at him.

'You also have friends who put vodka in the fruit punch, Tom,' Josey couldn't help pointing out.

'That was an accident,' he said. 'I hadn't told them I was on medication, anyway.'

'Your father and I don't know each other very well,' Josey put in, thinking that she had to help Guy explain. 'We haven't actually known each other long.'

'Don't threaten, Tom,' Guy said. 'It's not appropriate— especially now.'

'It isn't a threat, just a statement of fact. I don't want you acting like a martyr to my illness,' Tom went on, his voice shaking now. 'How do you think that makes me feel? Maybe I'll have this for the rest of my life, so I don't want you as a doddering old man, searching the city for me every time you don't know where I am.'

'Point taken, Tom,' Guy said, with an amazed, sobered note in his voice. He reached forward and placed a hand over Tom's hand. 'You've sure put me in my place.'

'You see, Dad, I'm not some passive thing that has to be acted upon all the time. I'm capable of acting, too,' Tom went on, his face red with a certain embarrassment. 'I know that several people, and Josey, saved my life last night, and I'm sure grateful…but I still feel the same.'

There was a silence. Neither Josey nor Guy wanted to say anything more then; there was nothing to say that wouldn't have sounded trite. Both Tom himself and Guy must be thinking, as she was, of the time he had gone out into the cold inadequately clothed when he had been depressed. That time he had come back. Would he always come back?

'I know I'm sick, Dad, but I do have normal times when I can see what's happening to other people...to you. I'm not totally focussed on myself,' Tom said.

'I never thought you were totally focussed on yourself, Tom,' Guy said quietly, while Josey looked down, feeling this interaction to be between father and son, although indirectly pertaining to her as well, 'but what you're saying is particularly ironic in light of what happened last night, even though it was an accident. It's not in my nature to abandon responsibilities, or abandon people.'

'I know that, but you can relax a bit, Dad, because I'm growing up. I know you married Mum to "save" her. I know that made you feel good, and you did save me and Rachel from a tacky life, you gave us love...but Mum is pretty ditzy anyway. She would have gone to hell with any man, no matter how strong or good. I can see all that now. She's just an inadequate person,' Tom said. 'I've had a long time to think about those things. Like all my life. Josey isn't like her, I can tell.'

'Point taken, Tom,' Guy repeated, while Josey sat there, impressed.

'You can't help those people beyond a certain point, I've realized. I guess I sort of accept her just the way she is...pretty hopeless. And I don't really want her in my life.' Tom paused and looked directly at Guy. 'I love you, Dad, but don't make me responsible for *your* lack of a life.'

Josey looked imploringly at Guy. 'Should I leave?' she asked. 'This is really private between you two.'

'No, don't leave,' Tom said. 'Why don't you two get married? That would be the best thing for my dad. He needs a woman like you, and he's a pretty good catch.'

In spite of the embarrassment of it, the heat that had come over her entire body, Josey couldn't help laughing, not looking at Guy. She knew that her face was flaming. 'I…er…I'm not sure I'm looking for a catch, Tom,' she said, smiling, 'but I do think you have a lot of very valid points.'

'Yeah…well,' Tom said, hesitating at last, 'sometimes you can think too much, and not do anything.'

A few minutes later, Josey and Guy stood in the corridor outside Tom's room, a little way down. It was time for Josey to go to the locker room in the ER to change for her work shift.

'He's very articulate, isn't he?' Josey remarked, very conscious of the two spots of high colour still on her cheeks. 'I guess that has put us both in our place with regard to him.'

'Yes, he always was articulate,' Guy agreed wryly, with an apologetic grin, 'but never quite as much as that. At the risk of sounding hokey, maybe he's got me figured out better than I know myself.'

'Yes, perhaps,' she agreed. The heightened awareness between them was almost unbearable to Josey, whose emotions vied between the need to escape and the desire to be with Guy. It was in some ways a relief that she had to go to work in a few minutes.

'Um…what will you do now?' she said.

'Stay with him a bit longer,' he said, 'to make sure he's not upset. We'll talk some more.'

'He has a point,' she said carefully. 'Several, in fact.'

'Yes. May I call you tomorrow, Josey?' It seemed to her there was determination in his tone as he stood next to her, a tall, handsome man, somehow humbled. A frisson of anticipation went through her, as though the outburst of the son had given the father permission to think of himself. Would he take up that challenge?

Josey looked at her watch. 'Must go, Guy,' she murmured. 'Good luck.' Standing on tiptoe, she kissed him on the cheek, and he caught her round the waist and pulled her against him in the quiet corridor where there was no one else about at that moment.

Fiercely he kissed her on the mouth. 'Perhaps I'd better act the role he's assigned for me,' he said wryly when he broke away, his eyes dark with an awareness of her. 'Maybe we should get together, as he suggested. I can think of a few ways I would like to get together with you, Josey.' He smiled at her wickedly and it was good to see him relax a little.

'If you want to, Guy,' she dared to say, knowing that she would escape in a moment.

'I do,' he said.

Agitated, she hurried away, not looking back. They were always so rushed, everything in her life was so rushed. If only they had time together to get to know one another more, to relax and do nothing.

She hoped for a steady stream of work, nothing dramatic, until her shift ended at half past eleven, to take her mind off Guy and Tom. He had said some time ago that any initiative must come from her—but she had no idea where to begin—no idea at all. Now, unexpectedly, the son had precipitated something. One thing she was sure of was that the influence of Joe seemed to be dying a natural death, and she was hardly noticing its passing.

Next morning Josey woke up suddenly, forced into consciousness by the sound of a car outside stuck in snow, the whine of its engine breaking into her sleep. Momentarily disorientated, she looked at her bedside clock to see that it was 9 a.m. Although it was light outside, a glimmer coming through the closed curtains, the light had that grey, murky quality of winter that made her want to hibernate.

It was Monday, a blessed day off, so with a sigh of relief and pleasure she snuggled down further under the pile of blankets and the down duvet, pulling it up over her ears. She could stay in bed all day if she wanted to, all night as well, and all the next day. Smiling to herself, thinking about Guy, she drifted back into sleep.

When the telephone on the bedside table rang, jerking her into wakefulness again, she saw that the time was just after 11 a.m. Contemplating not answering it, she finally lifted the receiver after six rings.

'Josey,' Guy said, not waiting for her to identify herself. 'I want to see you. I couldn't wait any longer.'

Propping herself up on one elbow, she came to greater wakefulness. 'I…I'm still in bed,' she said, her mouth dry and her heart beginning to pound.

There was something in his voice, a decisiveness, a need, that she hadn't heard before, and she recognized it because it was in her, too, a sense of having come to the end of waiting. It was as though Tom's outburst had given them permission. Yet she was frightened, not knowing what to do.

There were a few seconds of silence. 'That's all right,' he said. 'Can I come anyway?' She knew he was asking her more than the obvious, making it easy for her.

'Yes,' she said, her voice coming out as a whisper. She cleared her throat. 'Where are you?' It was obvious from muted background street sounds that he was either calling from a public or a mobile phone.

'I'm actually standing on your front doorstep, Josey,' he said.

'What?' she exclaimed breathlessly, jerking more fully upright in the bed. 'You…you can't mean that.'

'I do. Can you come down to let me in?'

'Well…yes, but I'm not dressed…' Suddenly she felt overwhelmed, very wide awake now, trembling with a fear and anticipation. Fear that she wouldn't be what he wanted?

'That's all right,' he said again, his voice husky and indistinct. 'Don't get dressed. Just come down and let me in, Josey. I've taken the day off—two days, in fact. It's cold out here.'

Josey got up quickly and put on a dressing-gown. Why was it that the things you really wanted in life you were seldom really prepared for, often given little warning about? She raked a brush though her hair, staring at her sleepy face, devoid of make-up, in her dressing-table mirror. In the grey light of her room, the curtains closed, she could just make out her reflection—the pupils of her eyes were wide, her lips were parted in anticipation.

With her feet bare she padded down the staircase, hoping that her housemates, Donna and Mike, were both at work. A blast of arctic air came into the tiny hallway as she opened the door to let Guy in.

'I expect I woke you,' he said by way of apology as he entered and filled the space so that she felt dwarfed by him, very feminine and petite beside him in her silky nightdress and dressing-gown as she brushed against him to get the door closed. She moistened her dry lips with her tongue, feeling a constriction of nervousness in her throat as his astute eyes went over her, taking in her loosely fastened gown which gaped at the neck and showed her bare feet at the bottom.

'Yes, but it doesn't matter,' she said quickly. 'Um…is everything all right? With Tom?''

He nodded. 'Yes, he's good. He'll be coming home

maybe tomorrow. We want to get his medication sorted out, decide whether he can go without it.'

They stood looking at each other in the cool hallway. The atmosphere seemed to crackle with emotion and tension, the tension of desire and need. Josey felt that she was having trouble breathing. Slowly Guy's eyes travelled over her again.

'You look very sweet. I've often wondered what you would look like in bed,' he said huskily, then smiled slowly as her face flamed. 'And I do like the way you blush. Not many women seem to manage it. Sorry I woke you.'

'It's all right.'

'I've decided to take some much-needed time off, and the hospital has strict instructions not to let Tom discharge himself. It's unlikely that he would now, but I'm not taking any chances, in spite of what he said to both of us. Rachel has gone to stay with friends for a few days, by way of a break,' he said. 'Mrs Canning is still going to the house every day.' He was telling her that he really was free, for a short time. It was up to her to take advantage of that, if she wanted to.

Josey swallowed nervously. 'I…I see,' she said, looking at him with eyes that, she knew, had grown enormous as his gaze went over her face, taking her in, as though he hadn't seen her for a long time.

'Aren't you going to invite me in?' he said.

'Oh…yes…of course,' she said. 'I live upstairs.' She started up the stairs ahead of him, and he closed the staircase door behind him.

Very conscious of him right behind her, of her own nakedness under the flimsy outer coverings, she stumbled at the top step and he put out a hand to steady her. 'Don't be frightened of me, Josey,' he said.

On the top landing he put his hands on her upper arms, looking at her intently.

'I'm not,' she said. 'More likely, I'm frightened of myself, what I'll do. I...don't know how to behave.'

'Why?' he said softly.

'You said that any initiative had to come from me. That's not fair.' She managed to get the words out.

Guy reached forward and put a hand, a cold hand, at the back of her neck, caressing her skin with his thumb, moving his fingers up into her hair, a gesture that seemed to her—starved of love as she was—excessively intimate, and she closed her eyes as waves of pleasure sensitized her body to his presence. As though automatically, she turned her head and placed her lips on the bare skin of his wrist.

'I know it wasn't fair,' he said. 'I won't hold you to that if it's something you don't want. I seem to have taken it from you anyway. May I take my coat off? Can I stay?'

He spoke softly, the words having a mesmerizing effect on her, so that she could only nod. He took off his coat and boots, looking around for somewhere to put the coat so that she took it from him and, moving as though in a dream, put it on a chair in her sitting room.

Opposite, the bedroom door gaped open, showing her cosy double bed, the covers in disarray. There was something inviting about a bed that had just been slept in. Guy turned his head to look at it, then he took her hand and led her in there, into the semi-darkness, closing the door behind them. Her heart was pounding so much that it seemed to be right in her throat, and every part of her was now sensitized to him, so much so that she felt she might faint.

There was a slight air of apology about him that melted her heart. Here was a man who would not take her for granted, assuming that she was 'available'.

'I want to make love to you,' he said, standing in front

of her, only inches away so that she could feel his body warmth. He wore a check shirt under a sweater, and grey trousers that clung to his long legs, showing the hard muscles underneath. Josey stared at him, wanting to touch him but not having the courage to make a move. 'You can say no if you want to, Josey. You know that. I hope you won't say it.'

Perhaps it was the very fact that he didn't touch her just at that moment, but stood back waiting for her to decide, that made her realize she couldn't say no, couldn't let him turn and walk away from her out into the cold. More than anything she wanted to be crushed in his arms.

'I don't want to say no,' she managed to get out. 'But I'm frightened to let myself go.'

'I think you said that before,' Guy countered softly, reasonably, smiling. 'Don't be frightened, it's going to be all right. I have to be honest with you and myself that I can't just settle for the "pleasant" company—not with you, Josey. I want you so much, I'm going mad.'

'Oh, Guy,' she whispered, moving closer to him, looking up into his face. Never had he looked so attractive to her, his eyes dark with his desire for her, his expression tender and intense. He seemed to relax as he took her whispered words as a sign of assent.

His hands were on her shoulders, pushing away the dressing-gown from them. It slid to the floor and settled round her feet, revealing to him her silk nightdress, very feminine, trimmed with lace. With a sigh he came close against her, putting his lips to her forehead gently. Josey stood rigid, wanting him so much. When his hand touched her waist she jumped convulsively and he laughed softly. As he kissed her forehead, moving his mouth here and there on her hypersensitive skin, she closed her eyes, blotting out everything but his touch, trying to breathe normally and not hold her breath.

The hand on her waist moved upwards to her breast, and he placed his palm flat against her softness to move his hand gently over her. Keeping her eyes firmly shut, she swayed involuntarily against him and he put his other arm round her waist, holding her to him. At last she put her arms up around his neck and lifted her face for him to kiss her. Very gently his mouth captured hers.

At the point where she felt she could bear it no longer, when she felt she was on the point of begging him to make love to her, he pulled back and took both her hands in his and stood looking at her, his face sensual with his desire for her. Now she felt more relaxed and compliant, thinking only of him in the cosy enclosed world of her bedroom.

It was then that she became aware that his hands were trembling, and she felt curiously humbled. It was obvious that he at least wanted her as much as she wanted him; she didn't have to hold back, to pretend a modesty and coolness. 'Oh, Guy,' she whispered. 'I'm glad you came.'

What had seemed like a very long wait was over. He undid the tiny mother-of-pearl buttons on her nightdress and smoothed it away from her shoulders so that it, too, fell to the floor, then his hands moved over her, arousing her to every nuance of him. 'You're so lovely.' He murmured the words against her hair, his breathing uneven. 'I want to spend the day with you here. Is that all right?'

'Yes.' She walked over to the bed and got under the covers, her legs trembling so that she felt clumsy. Suddenly she was shy of her nakedness, and impatient to have him beside her. Taking the initiative, she held out a hand to him.

Seated beside her on the bed, he undressed, then swung

himself in beside her, pulling her down with him. 'Before you came here,' she said, 'I wanted to hibernate.'

'Good,' he said, his voice thick, lying down beside her, gathering her against him. 'We can hibernate to-gether…later.'

The feel of his skin against hers was something she had dreamt about. The reality was so much more wonderful, her breasts brushing tantalizingly against the warmth of his chest, the nipples almost unbearably sensitized, her thighs pressed against the length of his as they lay side by side. Josey closed her eyes, her whole body tingling with plea-sure. All her life, it seemed, she had been waiting for Guy Lake.

In his arms she felt small, delicate and loved, not the super-competent Josey Lincoln, RN, who had to be always ready for anything that might present itself, having to be careful never to make a mistake because the consequences could be dire. For once she could give herself up to pure pleasure, let herself go.

'This is an act of faith, Josey,' he said.

Possessively he kissed her, demanding a response from her, which she gave in full measure, moving her body under his so that he supported his weight above her by leaning on his elbows, looking down into her face. They smiled at each other, slowly, sensually.

'Hello,' he said.

'Hello.'

Then she knew for sure that she loved him…

Throughout the day they slept and made love alternately, cocooned under the warm covers, as though it were the most natural thing in the world. They didn't talk much. Perhaps there had been enough talking between them for now, Josey thought sleepily as her limbs lay entwined with his, thinking that this was a good way to get a life, as Tom had said.

From time to time Guy telephoned the hospital on his mobile phone, asking about Tom or talking to Tom. As Josey lay with her eyes closed she heard him also speaking quietly to Rachel, and to Mrs Canning.

When early evening came she got up and prepared them something to eat, which she brought into the bedroom on a tray. When they had eaten, he took off the dressing-gown with which she had covered herself and folded her in his arms. Later, he left her for a while to visit his son.

They stayed together all night, all of Tuesday and most of that evening. When he at last stood at the door of her apartment to leave her, large in his outdoor clothing, she knew that his absence would dominate her every moment from now on.

'Will you come on holiday with us? With me, Rachel and Tom?' he asked her. 'In the March school holiday we go to Barbados for the two weeks. I rent a house on a beach, the same one. It's a great place. That will give us an opportunity to get to know one another better…you and me, and the other two. We need to get away from winter.'

'I would love to,' she said honestly, delightedly. 'I've never been there. I…I'll have to see if I can get the time off at such relatively short notice. You know how it is, we have to book our time off months in advance.'

'I'll have to twist Mac's arm, if necessary.' He grinned down at her. 'I'm a little bigger than she is.'

Josey laughed at the imagery. 'You do that,' she said, unaccustomed happiness settling on her like a warm cloak. 'And, Guy, thank you for coming here. I'm so glad that you did.'

'So am I ,' he said significantly, giving her a kiss on the

tip of her nose. 'I'm curious about something, my love—what do you think now about Joe Falconer?'

'I...' Josey began.

'For a few seconds,' he said softly, 'the expression on your face was quite blank, as though you didn't know who I was talking about. I feel gratified by that. I want you to forget him.'

Josey laughed, knowing for certain now that she loved this man with all her heart, with a love of an entirely different quality to what she had felt for Joe, when she had felt fearful a lot of the time, treading on eggshells, as it were. With Guy there would be an equality she had longed for. It all seemed like a wonderful dream, one where she had her eyes wide open.

'I'm beginning to forget what he looks like,' she said, smiling. She wanted to tell Guy that she loved him, but shyness held her tongue-tied. Plenty of time for that, all the time in the world.

'That's exactly what I want to hear,' he said. 'Come down to the door with me.'

When he had gone she ran upstairs and flung herself on the bed, burying her face in a pillow that bore the scent of his cologne, wanting to laugh and cry. She hadn't told him she loved him, it was too premature. Neither had he said anything to her, yet the knowledge of it had been there between them as a quiet certainty. It would come...it would come.

In the middle of March they lay on sand shaded by a cluster of palm trees, the heat caressing their bare skins and dispelling all reality of winter back home. Not far away the surf of the Caribbean Sea landed and receded in hypnotic rushes. On that part of the beach there were few other people, as the garden of the house, with a fence, hedge and trees, bordered the pale sand and a wooden private deck that belonged to the property.

Josey had her eyes closed, delighting in the play of light and shadow that danced over her face and bikini-clad body from the sunlight peeping through the waving palm fronds above her. Her hand lay loosely in Guy's grasp, her head turned towards him. Rachel and Tom, both turning a healthy biscuit colour in the sun, had just wandered up the beach in search of lunch from a beach-side shack café and to find the source of the steel band music they could hear faintly. If nothing else good happened to her in her life, Josey contemplated sleepily, this holiday would be like a perfect capsule of time.

Over the past weeks she had come to know Guy's children well, had been to their home for supper, had helped to cook. Tom's condition had stabilized, so that he had come out of the depression and was doing well at school. He had stopped taking off unannounced. Josey considered that her growing relationship with their father was having a very positive effect on both Tom and Rachel.

Guy let go of her hand and touched her thigh, gently caressing her with his fingers. After a few moments she got up, picked up her beach bag and languidly walked back into the garden through the wooden gate that stood open. Knowing that Guy was behind her, she went into the house, into their bedroom. As she took off her bikini, he came in behind her and locked the door.

Several times a day they made love, as well as at night, as though making up for years of drought. They couldn't stop making contact, touching, looking at each other. Sometimes Tom and Rachel exchanged indulgent glances, rolling their eyes, so that Josey blushed. She was getting used to those two young people, liking them a lot.

On the bed she opened her arms to Guy, impatient for him, and he came down beside her, already aroused.

'Mmm.' As their bodies joined together once again, he groaned with pleasure on a long sigh. 'I'll never get enough of you.'

Josey wrapped her limbs around him, burying her head against the hollow between his shoulder and his neck, still shy to show the ecstasy she knew was clear on her face. She had never known that making love could be like this. As attracted as she had been to Joe, she had always felt a sense of being 'on duty' with him, a sense of having to be something very specific that he wanted, having to perform in a certain way because otherwise he wouldn't be satisfied.

'I love you…I love you.' That was the first time she had actually said it. There was no point in not saying it now—she knew that through her haze of joy in the moment. Whatever came of it, she wanted him to know.

They slept for a while, then dozed, listening to the sound of the sea. 'I'm going to make tea,' Guy announced, kissing her, then swinging his legs off the bed to reach for his shorts from the floor.

While he was out, Josey got a clean pair of shorts and an oversized lightweight T-shirt from a drawer and went into the adjoining bathroom to have a shower. As she was drying herself afterwards she caught sight of herself in the full-length mirror and her attention was arrested by what she saw. There was something different about her, she realized with a jolt of wonder. Not daring to speculate too much at first, she stared at her breasts, which looked larger than usual, heavy, more rounded…and there were prominent blue veins, like a fine network of lace, beneath the pale surface of her skin.

She cupped her hands under her breasts. They felt heavy and warm, and tender to the touch, as she had noticed when she had taken Guy's weight on her. Slowly she turned and sat down on the edge of the bath. When you had never been pregnant it wasn't at once evident, yet she felt a certainty that brought a strange feeling of joy to her. They hadn't used contraceptives, as though by silent, mutual consent, apart from the 'act of faith' remark Guy had made that first time. What would he think? She sat there as though stunned, a towel around her shoulders, hunched.

'Hey, the tea's here,' he called, knocking on the bathroom door.

'Coming,' she said, forcing a normal tone to her voice, when she wanted to shout and scream with hysterical joy. When she had finished drying herself she dressed in the shorts and T-shirt, then pulled her wet hair back into a ponytail.

They drank the tea with the tray on the bed between them. Later they would walk along the beach in the early evening when the heat of the sun had diminished, the best time of the day. Gresham General Hospital seemed very far away in every sense, another world.

Guy sat looking at her, cradling his mug of lemon tea in both hands. He looked nervous and, loving him as she did, Josey sensed what was coming. Coupled with the growing conviction that she was pregnant, Josey dared to let herself feel the joy that he was going to bring her.

'I want you to know that I love you and want to marry you,' he said. 'I'm saying it now in a moment of relative calm.' They smiled at each other. 'I think we would be good for each other, Josey. We understand each other's work, we know where we're coming from. More than anything else, I want to be with you always.'

Josey bit her lip, the tears starting in her eyes. She got up to go and sit beside him. She didn't have to say anything—he could see from her face that she loved him, that she wanted him. They sat and smiled at each other, holding hands.

'Maybe at the end of the summer, so that we have time to sort ourselves out? Hmm?' There was still anxiety in his eyes as he looked at her. It was nice not to be taken for granted, even now.

'I...' she wanted to tell him that she thought she was pregnant, but the words wouldn't come out properly. 'The thought of not being with you is unbearable. I love you.'

'You would have to take on my children—until they're mature enough to leave home,' he said, still with an air of sounding her out, while his handsome face broke into a grin of joy.

'I could do that,' she ventured slowly. 'I like them a lot. And...Guy? You...er...would have to take on my child as well.'

'*What?*' He looked mystified for a few seconds, then slowly his expression turned to one of delight. 'You mean...?'

'Yes, I think so.' They were grinning at each other, then they flung their arms around each other and gripped tightly.

'Do you mind?' she asked rather unnecessarily, her anxiety giving way to unadulterated joy.

'I'm delighted...darling,' he said, covering her hands with his. 'And you?'

'Yes,' she said softly.

'Does that mean you will marry me?'

'Yes...yes. Yes, please.'

Later, Guy went out to find a drugstore that sold pregnancy testing kits, while Josey prowled around the house like a caged lion, not able to concentrate on anything else. Outside in the garden Rachel and Tom entertained some new-found friends of their own ages who were staying in a villa just along the beach. They hadn't yet noticed her agitation and abstraction—no doubt that would come later.

When Guy came back with a pregnancy kit, she went to the bathroom and locked the door.

'It's positive!' She came out with a stunned look on her face. 'It's really positive!' Then the tears came, falling silently down her cheeks. 'Oh, Guy, I'm going to have your baby. Hold me.'

Josey reached for him and he held her tightly, rocked her. 'Your baby, too, my darling,' he said joyfully. 'Ours.'

'I can hardly believe it,' she whispered.

'We'll go along to the beach hut for supper later,' Guy said. 'We'll dance to steel band music, then we'll tell Rachel and Tom. I'll tell them we're getting married, if you'll tell them about the baby. Right?'

Josey scrubbed at her face with the back of her hand. 'Right,' she said, smiling through her tears.

When they sat in the beach shack, which was open to the air, protected from rain only by thatch made of palm branches, Guy told the children during a lull in the music. They rolled their eyes again and chorused 'About time!' so loudly that a few people turned to look at them.

When Josey then told them that they were going to have a baby, they shouted 'About time!' again. They all became almost hysterical with laughter, then the steel band struck up again in the makeshift bandstand next to a small concrete dance floor at the side of the shack.

Guy stood up, extending a hand to Josey. 'Will you dance?' he said.

'You know,' he said against her ear, 'I shall be eternally grateful to Alec Ramsay for breaking a leg.'

'Yes,' she said dreamily. 'But for that I might never have

known you existed. What a waste. Shall we send him a postcard?'

'Let's.'

In each other's arms they swayed in time to the music. Never so happy, she knew that life wouldn't be easy, it never was, but with two on the same side it would be better than most. This was the first day of a new beginning, the first day of the rest of their lives...

# MILLS & BOON®

*Makes any time special*™

*Mills & Boon publish 29 new titles every month. Select from...*

Modern Romance™          Tender Romance™

Sensual Romance™

Medical Romance™  Historical Romance™

MAT2

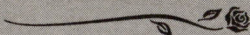